Mi

BEST SELLER ROMANCE

A chance to read and collect some of the best-loved novels from
Mills & Boon—the world's largest publisher of romantic fiction.

Every month, two titles by favourite Mills & Boon authors will
be republished in the *Best Seller Romance* series.

Penny Jordan

MARRIAGE WITHOUT LOVE

MILLS & BOON LIMITED
ETON HOUSE   18–24 PARADISE ROAD
RICHMOND   SURREY TW9 ISR

*First published in Great Britain 1981
by Mills & Boon Limited*

© Penny Jordan 1981

*Australian copyright 1981
Philippine copyright 1982
Reprinted 1982
This edition 1987*

ISBN 0 263 75938 5

*Set in Monophoto Baskerville 11 on 11½ pt
02–1187*

*Printed and bound in Great Britain by
Collins, Glasgow*

CHAPTER ONE

It was quite a long way from the canteen to the office of the Editor of the *Daily Globe*, especially when one was carrying a tray holding two tea cups, a pot of tea, milk and sugar, but Briony Winters was used to it. Her small, slight frame belied her strength just as her soft, feminine features belied her nature.

She pushed open the door of the outer office, which was hers, noticing with a frown the heavy masculine topcoat flung carelessly over the spare chair. Doug Simons, her boss, often had visitors, but very few of them wore coats like that. It was wool, and expensive, meticulously tailored and lined in silk. Briony put down the tray, wondering about whether to give up her own cup for the visitor, when she realised that the inner door was not quite closed.

'Well, you'll have no problems with the job, of course,' Doug was saying. 'Not after working on the *Telegraph*.'

'Which, I take it, means I could have in other areas.'

Although the man's voice was faintly muffled, there was no mistaking its hard inflexibility, and Briony frowned, her lips drawing together in a cold line.

'Well, it's just Briony . . .'

The very mention of her own name should have been sufficient to send her out of earshot, but despite allegations among the male staff of the paper to

5

the contrary, Briony was only human.

'Briony?'

Again that note of sharp query.

'Briony Winters, my secretary,' Doug supplied. 'Well, your secretary now. She might give you a hard time at first . . . until she gets used to you.'

'*She* might . . .? My God, no wonder your sales are slipping if you allow your secretary to dictate to you, Doug!'

The coolly insolent words made Briony's fingers curl angrily into her palms. For two pins she'd march right into Doug's office and demand to know exactly why he thought it necessary to explain to his replacement that he might have 'problems'. Didn't she fulfil her secretarial duties with a good deal more efficiency and effectiveness than any of the other secretaries?

She had been away on a fortnight's holiday when the news of Doug's promotion broke and had come back to find the paper in an uproar, with Doug due to leave for New York only three days after his replacement arrived. Since the *Globe* had been taken over by an American newspaper group, such transatlantic moves had become commonplace, and Briony hadn't been unduly surprised to hear that Doug's replacement was from the States. She herself didn't particularly like American men. They were inclined to be brash and noisy. And worse, they didn't know· when to take 'no' for an answer. She stared angrily at the door. Doug had no right . . . no right at all to discuss her like this.

'What is she?' she heard the other man say sardonically. 'Some sort of female dragon? A Women's Libber with her hair in a bun and thick ankles?'

'No way,' Doug said dryly. 'As it happens, she's got one of the sexiest bodies I've ever seen.'

Outside the door Briony writhed in furious resentment. Doug had never given the slightest inkling that he had even noticed her body, and if he had she wouldn't have continued to work for him.

'Woe betide you if you try to touch it, though,' Doug was warning his companion. 'Briony has a hang-up where men are concerned. She can't stand them, and it isn't a sham. Something to do with something that happened in her teens.'

'A teenage romance goes wrong and turns her into a man-hater? Come on, Doug. These are the nineteen-eighties!'

'Well, some people take things harder than others. I'm just warning you to take things easy. She's the best secretary I've ever had—works hard and is meticulously efficient.'

'Maybe so,' the hard voice said curtly. 'But if she wants the kid glove treatment she shouldn't be working on a paper. Secretaries are expendable, Doug,' the man added in a bored voice, 'even the best of them.'

Briony gripped her desk, her voice white with fear and shock. There had been redundancies on the paper the summer before and she had been terrified, then, that she might lose her job. It was something she daren't even contemplate. She depended on it too heavily. It paid well, and Doug had always been flexible about hours, which had been an added bonus. But now Doug was leaving and she would be working for a man she had already decided she hated, without even meeting him. He was still talking to Doug, and she moved away from the door on legs suddenly weak and trembling. Whoever he was, he was no American. His accent was English. She could tell that even though his voice was muffled by the door.

The intercom buzzed and she flicked it down, her voice coolly remote as she answered Doug.

'Come into my office for a moment, would you, Briony?' he requested. 'There's someone here I'd like you to meet.'

There was a small mirror on the wall behind her, but she didn't bother to look in it. She stood up picking up her notebook and pencil through sheer force of habit, a small girl, with a mane of dark red hair that curled thickly round a perfectly oval face. Her skin was pale and creamy; almost translucent. She had delicate features and large green eyes which looked as though they might once have been vulnerable but which now reflected only the image of whoever looked into them. Looking into Briony's eyes was like looking at a one-way mirror, from the wrong side, one of her infuriated male colleagues had once said. The only time anyone saw any expression in them was if some man tried to sexually belittle her. Then they filled with bitterness and contempt. Slender to the point of fragility, there was a steel-like quality about her, a coldness which allowed no one to trespass close enough to discover the woman she might be beneath the layers of ice in which she was encased. She was twenty-three and as composed as a woman ten years older. 'Frigid' and 'incapable of feeling were just two of the many insults frustrated males had hurled at her, but they pleased rather than offended. Where men were concerned her emotions were completely burnt out, leaving nothing but bitter hatred.

Despite that, Doug was envied his secretary. She was cool, and calm, and could be relied on completely in an emergency. Her job was no sinecure. She was on the go from nine until six every day, working late quite often, and always ready to work through a lunch-hour or give up free time if it was necessary. The other girls joked that she didn't have a private life, and that the paper was her family; and although they were reluctant to admit it, most of them felt slightly in awe of her.

As she pushed open the door Doug smiled at her. Doug Simons was in his mid-fifties, a power-house of human energy, who had worked in newspapers since he left school. He and Briony got on very well—or at least she had thought they had until she heard him discussing her so freely. Happily married with a grown up family and a wife on whom he doted, he represented no threat to her defence systems. Neither did he constantly annoy her with unwanted sexually based conversation or false flattery of a type insulting to both her intelligence and her taste. Men thought they only had to smile and wheedle and girls would gladly jump into bed with them. Well, not her!

Doug smiled warmly at her, his expression faintly ingratiating as though he was half afraid of what she might do or how she would react.

She smiled back—a slight widening of warmly curved lips to show even white teeth, the smile not reaching her eyes, which remained as clear and cold as glass.

Doug's companion had his back to her. He didn't turn to look up at her, nor did he betray any other awareness of her presence, and she prickled with animosity. His hair was dark and thick, brushing the collar of the expensive suit he was wearing, and she stiffened as warily and antagonistically as a cat faced with a large, threatening dog.

'Kieron, meet your new secretary, Briony. Briony—Kieron Blake.'

She at least had had the advantage of hearing his name, and thus the precious gift of a few seconds to prepare herself. He had had nothing, and she observed the shocked incredulity of his expression with grim satisfaction. Navy-blue eyes swept slowly and disbelievingly over her; looking for the scars? she asked herself bitterly. He wouldn't find any. She had concealed them all too well.

'Briony?' His eyebrows rose in contemptuous accusation, and although inwardly terrified, Briony refused to be drawn. Let him think what he liked. He hadn't changed. The long-boned Celtic face was still as physically compelling; the high cheekbones and harsh male features still as disturbing. His skin was tanned, the thick dark hair worn slightly longer than she remembered, and the suit more formal. He had himself under control now, the shock carefully masked, only the faint clenching of his jawbone revealing the control he was having to exert.

'Kieron's going to need all the help you can give him until he settles in, Briony,' Doug told her, sublimely unaware of the undercurrents eddying fiercely around him. 'I'm going to take him round and introduce him to the other editors and then we're going out to lunch. Anything urgent, get Phil to deal with it, will you?'

Phil Masters was Doug's assistant, a tall gangly Scot with a shock of red hair and a temper to match.

Doug and Kieron were standing up, Kieron extending his hand to her, his expression a mingling of contempt and indifference, which changed to anger as she withdrew automatically from him.

With Doug looking on she could hardly make a scene, but the touch of those cool brown fingers against her own skin made her shake with a sickness and fear that left her drained and trembling. And this was only the beginning.

As she walked back into her own office, Kieron murmured something to Doug, and the connecting door was closed. Alarm prickled over her, fears she had thought long submerged suddenly filling her mind and obliterating everything else.

'How long has Briony worked for you?' Kieron asked Doug casually as the latter picked up his coat.

'Umm, about eighteen months. Best secretary I've ever had.' He hadn't been as unaware of Kieron's reaction to Briony as he had pretended, and naturally he was curious as to its cause. 'Am I right in thinking you know her?'

'I once thought I knew someone who looked like her, but it turned out that I didn't know her at all.'

His tone of voice warned Doug not to probe.

'I'm not surprised to hear she's a man-hater,' he added sardonically. 'She's one of those women who seem to get a thrill out of leading men on and then kicking them in the teeth. Quite a hang-up!'

Doug didn't argue the point. Whatever relationship had once existed between Briony and Kieron was their business and theirs alone, but he could foresee fireworks between them in the not too far distant future, if they were going to work together.

The two men emerged from the office, and Briony darted a quick look at Kieron's shuttered face. It told her nothing. When they had gone she stared unseeingly at her typewriter, ignoring the over-flowing 'in' tray, her mind racing frantically in circles as she tried to think of a way of ensuring that she need never set eyes on Kieron Blake again.

There wasn't one, of course. Not unless she gave up her job, and that was impossible. In a more buoyant economic climate she might have done so, even if it meant taking a drop in salary, but to take the risk in the middle of a depression would be extremely foolhardy. She needed her salary. Every penny of it. She closed her eyes, shivering suddenly with cold. The office door opened and she jerked upright, her face paper-white, but it was only Matt Dyson, one of the sub-editors. It was the joke of the *Globe* that while Briony gave every other male the cold shoulder, Matt Dyson, the original worm who never turned, was her only male escort.

'Is something wrong?' he asked, eyeing her with mingled uncertainty and embarrassment.

Doug referred unkindly to Matt as her 'lame dog', and it was true that his long face often wore an expression of anguished apology. He was nervous and introspective and the other men often made fun of him behind his back. He had once confided to Briony that he had wanted to become a painter, but that his parents had disapproved. He was in his late twenties, with fair, thinning hair, and mild hazel eyes. His wife had left him two weeks after Christmas, and now in April he still hoped every day that she would miraculously return to him. He worshipped the ground she trod, although Briony could not see why. Mary Dyson was a dumpy brunette, narrow-minded and everything that Briony disliked in her own sex. She had often contemplated telling Matt that his wife might treat him a little better if he treated her a little worse, but she had no intention of getting involved in other people's personal problems.

'Lunch with me?' Matt asked hesitantly. 'Or have you another date?'

She hadn't, and she didn't particularly feel like eating, but she knew that she could not remain in her office thinking about Kieron Blake.

To her surprise Matt took her to a fashionable new restaurant which had recently opened, and had become a favourite haunt of *Globe* staff. It was inclined to be rather pricey, and since she knew that Matt was having problems making ends meet, Briony frowned, wishing he had taken her somewhere more modest. Now she would have to insist on paying for her own meal and he would be hurt and offended.

The restaurant was full apart from one table set for six and one vacant, one for two next to it. The waiter removed Briony's coat with a flourish and a look in his eyes which immediately made her own harden as she directed a freezing stare at him.

Matt dithered over the menu. He always did, and Briony had grown used to it. In contrast she had decided what she was going to eat immediately, and she gave her order coolly, while Matt cast anguished glances, first at the menu and then at the hovering waiter. It took all of five minutes and they still had to endure the fiasco of choosing the wine. Matt

hadn't a clue about wine and normally ended up
hot and bothered and very obviously patronised by
the wine waiter. Briony sat through it all with
detached uninterest, throwing a cool smile at Matt
when he eventually managed to make up his mind,
which he accepted with the gratitude of a dog being
thrown a bone.

They had just started on their main course when
the table adjacent to them filled up. Briony was conscious of being scrutinised but refused to look up.
Matt turned to say something to her, and upset his
wine glass, an expression of abject apology on his
face as the contents cascaded over the table and
dripped on to her cream wool skirt. She stood up,
shaking off the moisture and assuring him that no
harm had been done. As she sat down again she
realised that the occupants of the other table were
Doug and Kieron, and four other deputy editors
from the paper.

Doug grinned at her, but it was Kieron Blake of
whom she was most aware, her hands shaking beneath the narrowed blue stare he turned upon her.

'Come and join us,' Doug invited, calling over a
waiter to move the tables together. 'We'll soon catch
up with you.'

Briony willed Matt to refuse, but of course he
didn't, and somehow she found herself sandwiched
beween Doug and Kieron while Matt sat opposite
her next to the Features Editor, Gail Wyndham.

Gail and Briony had never been particularly
friendly. Gail was a tall blonde, a career woman first
and foremost but one who made no secret of her
enjoyment of the opposite sex. It was rumoured that
she knew every attractive male on the *Globe* inti-

mately, and watching her openly flirting with Kieron Blake Briony suspected that it would not be too long before he joined that list. He was letting Gail make all the running, his manner lazily amused, just enough awareness in it to encourage her, and Briony felt faintly sick as she watched them together. One of the other men tried to engage her in conversation, but she cut him off abruptly, shocked to discover that Kieron had switched his attention from Gail to her, his eyes alert and watchful, a cynical twist to his lips.

'I've been dying to meet you for ages,' Gail murmured softly, stretching out a plum-tipped hand to touch his arm. 'You were quite a celebrity on the Street even before you went to the States.'

'Oh?'

Under the table Briony gripped her hands together until her knuckles showed white. From the moment she had seen Kieron Blake in Doug's office she had known this moment would come. It seemed ironic that after so many years of nightmares about it, the confrontation should arrive just when she had at last hoped she was over them. Inwardly she was shaking with mingled sickness and fear, but years of hiding her feelings and repressing them behind a blank wall helped her to concentrate on her food, although if anyone had asked her what she was eating she would not have had the faintest idea.

'The Myers case,' Gail continued in a husky voice. 'It made newspaper history—the sort of scoop we all dream about. While the rest of the press were speculating about what part of the world James Myers might have disappeared to, you managed to discover that he was right here in this country all the time, posing as his sister's boy-friend.'

'The Myers case?' Doug frowned. 'Wasn't he the crooked financier? The one who was reputed to have salted millions away?'

'Yes. It wasn't a very pleasant business,' Kieron said coolly. 'The man had been indulging in a form of legal robbery for years, but then he made a fatal slip and got found out. Everyone knew what was going on but no one could prove it, and before the police could build up a case against him it was rumoured that he'd skipped the country.'

'Only you knew differently,' Gail admired. 'How on earth did you find out the truth? By all accounts he was quite a master of disguise, and had been coming and going quite freely for weeks, posing as his sister's boy-friend.'

'Yes. He was hoping to leave the country when things had cooled down a bit. I had a few lucky breaks.'

'And a guillible informant, if all one hears is true,' Gail laughed. 'Didn't you get most of the detail for the story from Myers' sister's flatmate?'

'I never disclose my sources,' Kieron told her, smiling to soften the words. Briony could tell that Doug was impressed by this apparent show of loyalty and she could feel Kieron's eyes upon her across the width of the table, but she refused to look up. No matter what he might pretend to others, she knew the truth!

'In that case you didn't need to,' Gail said frankly. 'I wonder what on earth happened to that girl? There was some talk of her being tried as an accomplice at one stage.'

'*Tried*? but. . . .' Kieron caught himself up, but not

before Briony had observed his momentary shock with bitter satisfaction.

'Surely you knew?' Gail queried.

'As a newspaper editor you should know better than merely to assume the obvious,' Kieron parried.

Because he had no other defence against the question, Briony thought angrily.

'It was a very clever piece of reporting,' Doug observed, joining the conversation, his words jarring a nerve Briony had thought long dead.

'Clever?' she burst out before she could stop herself, her eyes burning with resentment, a loathing in her voice she did nothing to hide. 'Is that what you all think? That it's "clever" to destroy someone's life, just to get a front-page story? Well, I don't. I think it's despicable. Hateful!' She broke off, realising that the others were exchanging puzzled and amused glances.

'Come on, love, aren't you taking it a bit personally?' one of the other men commented. Briony knew Kieron was waiting for her to speak, but she couldn't. How could these cynical, worldly people understand the effect of their sophisticated moral code on others less worldly? And Kieron's attempts to pretend that he hadn't known. . . . That he had actually cared. . . . God, how she hated him!

'Something wrong, Briony?' Kieron asked her smoothly, giving her name faint emphasis. 'You don't seem to be enjoying your lunch.'

'The lunch is fine,' she retorted bleakly, 'but if you'll all excuse me, I've got work to do.' She glanced at Matt, not wanting to embarrass him in front of the others by offering to pay for her own lunch, and then shrugged the concern away. She could settle up with him later.

She had just walked past the table when she heard Gail say triumphantly, 'Beth Walker—that was the girl's name!'

Briony froze, her eyes dilating with fear, her hands cold and clammy.

'Beth Walker,' Kieron repeated softly, and Briony knew without looking at him that he was watching her.

She walked back to the office on legs which almost refused to support her, each breath a conscious effort. Her instinctive response was to grab her coat and leave before Doug and Kieron got back. But she could not.

On impulse she reached for a phone book, dialling the number of a well-known employment agency. The girl on the other end was helpful but regretful. In normal circumstances, she told Briony, they wouldn't have the slightest difficulty in placing her, but the way things were at the moment it might be months before they could find her a job which came anywhere near approaching her present highly paid one.

She slumped in her chair, not entirely surprised, wondering what on earth she was going to do. She felt as though her life had suddenly turned into a horrendous nightmare. Beth Walker. When she had discarded that name she had discarded the past, or so she tried to persuade herself, but it hadn't been easy. There were too many intrusive memories, too much that could not simply be forgotten. She had changed her name by deed poll after the attentions of the Press became too much to bear. It was ironic really that she should end up working for a newspaper. It had been from necessity rather than in-clination. She had needed a job that paid well, and employers who were prepared to take her on without digging too deeply into her past. Doug had taken her completely on trust, and for that alone she felt she owed him a debt which could never be entirely repaid. One had to experience the contempt and loss in faith of others before one could appreciate fully the value of trust.

She had once trusted Kieron Blake. And not just trusted him. Even now it made her feel sick to think how gullible she had once been.

The first time she had seen him had been at the flat she shared with Susan Myers. He had come, so he told her, to interview Susan for a gossip column article, and she had not been surprised, because al-though she and Susan lived together, their life styles were entirely different.

They had been brought up in the same small vil-lage. Susan was the spoiled and petted daughter of the local 'lord of the manor', Sir Arthur Myers, and his wife, and Briony had got to know her through her father who was their doctor. They had gone to school together, although never particularly inti-mate—Susan moved in a different, faster crowd, and it was only the death of Briony's parents within six months of one another—her father from a heart attack and her mother from a broken heart—that brought them together.

Briony's father was not a wealthy man. There were some investments and the house, which on her solicitor's recommendation Briony had sold. She had been contemplating going on to university after school, but fearing to use up her slender financial

resources had decided instead to invest in a good
secretarial course. It was then that Susan Myers,
chaffing under the parental yoke, suggested that they
'flat' together. Not that Susan was contemplating a
secretarial career. Her ambitions were nowhere near
as modest. Her long-suffering parents paid for her to
undergo an expensive modelling course from which
she emerged sleek and soignée; the occasional
modelling job and her father's allowance giving her
a far different life style from Briony's steady nine-to-
five routine. In fact long before her secretarial course
was over Briony was regretting her decision to share
with Susan. All-night parties; casual sexual morals;
these had no place in her life, but she was unable to
afford the expense of the flat without Susan and had
perforce to endure her presence.

Susan's brother she knew only by hearsay. Ten
years separated them, Susan being the child of Sir
Arthur's second marriage, and although Susan was
fond of boasting about her successful half-brother,
Briony had never met him. Nor had she wanted to,
disliking what she read about him in the Press, but
when the story had broken, no one had believed her
innocence, and the one person who could have sub-
stantiated it was missing.

Her mouth twisted bitterly. Kieron must have
thanked his lucky stars that Susan was so conveni-
ently missing that evening. She had told him when
the other girl would be in, but he had shown a flat-
tering disinclination to leave. They had talked—she
couldn't remember what about—only that for the
first time since her parents had died she didn't feel
completely alone. When he asked her out, she hadn't
even hesitated, and had never once suspected that

his questions were based on anything other than an interest in her own background. Later, of course, when the truth came out, she had realised that it was James Myers' background he had been seeking, not hers.

He had taken her out to dinner the evening they came back and found Susan and her new 'boy-friend' in the flat. Briony had put Susan's awkwardness down to the fact that she was merely playing one of her silly secretive games. Susan had a vivid imagination and liked to pretend her life was full of drama and suspense, but with hindsight she suspected that Kieron had known the truth right from the start.

It had said in the papers that James Myers was a master of disguise, and certainly it had never crossed Briony's mind that he was Susan's brother. He visited the flat quite often, and the two of them would retire to Susan's room, talking together in muted whispers. Whenever Kieron had asked about Susan and her 'boy-friend' Briony had innocently supplied the answers. She had even been the one to tell him that Susan was due to go abroad on a modelling trip, never dreaming that it was just a cover to smuggle James Myers out of the country on the false passport and documents he had had prepared.

Kieron had been particularly passionate that night. They had driven out of town and stopped at a small Thameside pub for a drink. It had been a long hot summer and she remembered she had been wearing a thin camisole top and a pretty cotton skirt. Kieron had traced the neckline of her top with one lazy finger, the casual caress sending her pulses racing with frightened excitement. How could anyone so attractive be interested in her? When he announced abruptly that they were leaving she had gone willingly. In the car he had pulled her to him, moulding her body against his own with a new intimacy that thrilled her. There had never been a second when she doubted his feelings. When he parted her lips in a passionate kiss she had responded without check, trusting him completely.

They had driven back to the flat in a silence which on her part was filled with tense excitement. Tonight was to be the climax to which their relationship had been slowly building. Her body felt curiously weightless, open adoration in her eyes as she turned them to her companion. She had remembered later how Kieron had stopped the car then, even though they hadn't reached the flat, his voice rough as he said unsteadily, 'Don't look at me like that. . . .'

And she, little fool that she was, had thought he meant that if she did he wouldn't be able to control himself! If only she had known! There hadn't been a single occasion during their association when he hadn't known exactly what he was doing, hadn't been completely and absolutely in control of everything, including her. Manipulating her like a jointed doll, and she had let him.

It was dark when they got back, and the flat was empty. Susan had gone home for the weekend. Her father hadn't been feeling well, and she had been furious when her mother phoned to beg her to return. She hated the country and seemed to have no feelings for her parents whatsoever.

The flat had been unpleasantly cool after the warmth of the car, and Briony had shivered slightly.

Kieron had removed his jacket, draping it round her slender shoulders, and laughing gently because it drowned her. Then the laughter had died and he had taken her in his arms, kissing her with a new demanding force that overwhelmed her. She remembered that she had protested slightly and said something about making them some coffee, but Kieron had laughed, and said no, he had other things in mind.

Somehow his hand had slipped beneath the flimsy camisole and was caressing her breast, the sudden passionate surge of her own flesh taking her off guard. She had gasped slightly, her eyes wide and wondering, wonder giving way to a totally different emotion when Kieron slid the thin strap down from her shoulder, placing his lips to the burgeoning flesh his hand had just vacated.

'You're beautiful,' he had told her slowly, his hands removing her clothes and his eyes doing incredible things to her emotions. She told herself that what she was doing was wrong, only her arguments were somehow less than convincing. How could the way she felt about Kieron ever be wrong? It was deliciously and passionately right.

She couldn't remember how they got into the bedroom, but she could remember, with vivid clarity, the hard warmth of Kieron's body against hers; the strangeness of his male flesh, and the aching sensation of intense need that seemed to start somewhere in the pit of her stomach and spread languorously all through her body.

Once, as his lips roved possessively over her skin, she protested, the small sound silenced as he cupped her face and kissed her lingeringly until there was no thought in her head but him.

He was beautiful, she had thought achingly, staring wonderingly at his body. He was like a Greek statue come to life, and she wanted to touch him and go on touching him for ever. As though he sensed what she was feeling he had guided her hands to his skin, murmuring soft encouragements whenever shyness made her hesitate.

The thought of his possession brought her no fear. His slow, expert lovemaking had expunged that, but what she had not expected was her own sudden passionate need, kindled by his touch and expertise, and pushing aside the barriers of innocence and inexperience.

When she arched against him, her fingers tensing into his back, he soothed her softly, driving her almost into a mindless frenzy of intolerable aching need, before finally parting her thighs with his full weight.

In confirmation of his greater experience he was ready for her sudden tremulous fear and clenching muscles, his hands steadying her and soothing her tension, as he kissed her softly, murmuring to her to relax. The pain was sharp and intense, and she cried out to him to stop, but her cry had been ignored and for a moment hurt and pain combined with outraged resentment to make her fight against his domination. But as though he had expected it, the rebellion was quelled, his body taking her through pain to pleasure—a pleasure such as she had never dreamed of, her cries of pain turning to soft moans of desire and those to hoarse, throbbing pleas for fulfilment.

She fell asleep in his arms, convinced that life

could hold no greater happiness, her limbs tangled sleepily and trustingly with his. She felt no shame for what had happened. It had been natural and beautiful and she was filled with gratitude for his patience and skill. Her last conscious thought was that she could not imagine what she had ever done in her life to deserve him.

In the morning she felt exactly the same thing, but in a totally different context. While she slept, wrapped in pleasurable dreams, Kieron had searched the flat, and found, as he expected, the evidence of James Myers' duplicity. He had managed to get the paper to hold the front page for him, but Briony did not see it until she got to work.

The article caught her eye while she was taking off her coat, and recognising the Myers name she had started to read it, work forgotten as numb, appalled realisation swept over her. The article bore Kieron's name—as though he was proud of what he had done, she had thought bitterly. She had looked so ill that her boss had sent her straight home. When she reached the flat it was to find it besieged with reporters and police, and none of them had been gentle with her. 'Kieron Blake's informant,' was how one paper described her. Others were less kind. Susan had returned from the country with her parents. Sir Arthur had been deliberately cruel and remorseless, and at the end of the week her boss suggested that because of the notoriety, it might be as well if she found another job. She worked in a solicitors' office, and as he explained in great embarrassment, clients might not feel they could trust a firm which employed a girl known to have betrayed a friend's trust.

She had wanted to scream that it hadn't been like
that, but pride held her silent. Her only crime was
that she had believed herself loved; stupidly, crim-
inally, foolish of her perhaps, but she had not and
never would have breathed a word of anything that
might have deliberately been construed as breaking
a trust.

The police had questioned her for hours, and
when Sir Arthur died from a heart attack just before
the case came to court she had received an avalanche
of poison pen letters. That was when she had decided
to change her name.

For three months she had endured absolute hell,
and not once in all that time had she heard a word
from Kieron—neither of compassion, nor regret, not
even of acknowledgement of what he had done. She
had not tried to contact him. Pride alone had sustained her through the horror of it all, but her trust,
her faith, and her innocence were smashed beyond
repair.

The office door swung open, banishing the past.
She looked up quickly, her eyes freezingly disdain-
ful. Kieron had always been tall, but now he was
broader than she remembered, filling the small
space, his eyes deeply and darkly contemptuous as
they looked at the open telephone directory. One
lean finger ran smoothly down the page, stopping
unerringly against the number of the employment
agency.

'No luck?' he drawled sardonically. 'Too bad.'

Briony forced herself not to respond, her eyes
carefully blank as she removed the directory and put
a piece of paper in her typewriter.

'I'm sorry, Mr Blake.'

'*Mr* Blake?' he sneered coldly. 'Oh, come on, surely we needn't be so formal—*Beth!*'

The last word was said softly, almost a taunt, and Briony swung round, her eyes blazing with anger and contempt.

'Don't call me that!' she snapped.

'Why not? It's your name.'

'Not any longer,' Briony told him crisply. How dared he deliberately remind her of the past! 'I left it behind me.'

'How convenient.' Kieron had his back to her, his dark head bent over some papers, 'Tell me, *Briony*, did you bring anything of Beth with you, when you decided to trade personalities?'

'Not a thing,' Briony assured him shortly. Why was he plaguing her with these questions, resurrecting memories she would rather had remained forgotten?

'That's a pity. At least she was a warm, living, breathing woman.'

'Who you destroyed!'

The words were out before she could stop them, and Kieron's eyes narrowed sharply as he swung round and stared at her.

'What makes you say that?'

Sheer disbelief held her rigidly silent. How could he stand there and ask her that? Hadn't he deliberately and coldbloodedly used her, and then when he had got his story, simply dropped her? He knew how she had felt about him—she had never made the slightest attempt to hide it. He was an intelligent man; he must have known how she would react, how shocked and distressed she would be. She had learned from a photographer who had worked with him, and whom she had bumped into by accident three months after he had left, that his career was flourishing. He had been posted abroad somewhere, although where the photographer had not said.

'So, nothing of the Beth I knew remains?' Kieron persisted.

He was watching her intently and Briony felt like a helpless little fly being pursued by a particularly relentless spider. What did he want? An admission of how close he had come to completely destroying her, to gloat over?

'Nothing,' she told him emotionlessly.

His anger seemed to explode over her.

'Don't lie to me, Briony!' he gritted furiously, 'I saw your face when you walked into that office and saw me sitting there. You hate my guts, don't you. Don't you?' he demanded when she refused to answer.

'Haven't I the right?' Her hands were curled into two small fists. 'After what you did. . . .'

For a long moment he said nothing, merely watching her in a way that made Briony shiver with apprehension. Why should he examine her with such contempt? He was the one at fault. He was the one who. . . .

'You're quite right,' he said softly, cutting across her bitter thoughts. 'The Beth I knew has gone completely. You're quite a woman, aren't you, Briony? A woman of iron and steel, according to the office grapevine. The Beth I knew would never have held on to a grudge so tightly, nor become so bitter. But then the Beth I thought I knew never. . . .' He broke off and without warning leaned over her, watching her eyes spit defiance. It was only when he kept on coming, and Briony eventually shrank back, that she thought she saw some emotion flicker deep in the narrowed eyes, but it was gone almost instantly, his expression withdrawn as he said curtly, 'You're perfectly safe. You've made your point, but I don't intend working with a secretary who looks at me as though I've crawled out from under a particularly slimy stone. So if I were you I'd have another look at this.' He dropped the directory he had removed from the shelf behind her on to her desk with a derisive smile, and started to walk towards the door.

'One thing at least hasn't changed,' he said unkindly, pausing to watch the wary expression creep into her eyes. 'At least not if all the gossip one hears is correct. It seems you still enjoy turning men on and then freezing them off. With one notable exception.'

Briony gasped at the unfairness of the accusation, and the cynical, twisted smile which had accompanied his last words, and was just about to demand an explanation when Kieron added acidly:

'You've made how you feel about me quite plain, Briony. You hate and loathe me, right?'

When she didn't comment, he breathed out sharply, anger etched deep in his face.

'God, you must want to keep this job very badly!'

'Very badly,' Briony agreed coolly, hoping that her voice wouldn't betray anything that she was feeling. How on earth she was going to work for Kieron and keep her sanity she did not know, but work for him she must.

'So that you can be with Matt?'

Before Briony could get over the shock of the accusation, Kieron was saying with bitter contempt,

'Is that what your taste runs to these days? He's not a man, he's a babe in arms!'

Briony went white, but Kieron had already turned away. She fumbled for a piece of paper and put it in her typewriter, her fingers rattling over the keys in an even staccato rhythm, but the typewritten words were blurred by a mist of tears she was powerless to control.

CHAPTER TWO

IT was after seven when Briony stepped wearily off the bus at the end of her road. There had been a last-minute panic necessitating recall of an article and she had worked late to help Doug get the crisis sorted out. The adrenalin flow which had helped her through the day had abated, leaving her feeling drained and exhausted. Her feet dragged as she walked up the tree-lined avenue. It had been a perfect spring day, and now as long golden shadows fell across the pavement the last liquid notes of birdsong filtered sweetly through the air.

She had a long way to commute, but she had particularly wanted a house with at least some pretensions towards being rural. She knew North London wasn't fashionable and people raised their eyebrows when they discovered how far out of town she was, but the house had a long back garden, which was enclosed with hedges and boasted half a dozen wizened apple trees, and in the spring when they were in blossom and the cherry trees flowered along the surburban pavements she could almost convince herself it was as good as the country.

She had bought the house three years ago, a necessity rather than a luxury, and as well as realising her modest investments she had had to take on a seemingly huge mortgage. House prices had soared since the sale of her parents' old home, especially in London, and she had been desperate when she found this house. Split into two self-contained flats, it was ideal for what she needed and she occupied the lower flat, the upper being let to an Italian couple who were living in England on a temporary basis. They had a baby girl and Briony got on very well with them, especially Gina, who was her own age and very much on her wavelength.

Gina was waiting for her when she opened the front door, and her heart instantly started to pound with fear, her mouth dry with dread.

'Has . . . .'

'Everything is fine,' Gina soothed her fondly. 'Never have I known such an anxious mamma! It is because you cannot be with your child as you would wish. This I understand. I came down merely to get his night things, he is tired from playing in the garden. . . .'

Relief swept over her in a wave and she sagged against the door, her face white with strain. This was the penalty she must pay for being a working mother. Gina watched over Nicky as though he were her own child, she knew that, and yet always at the back of her mind was the consuming fear that something might happen to him through her inability to be with him; that he would need her and she would not be there. She was lucky to have Gina, she knew. The Italian couple had been desperate when they came to her, and she had let them have the flat at a very modest rent, but she had never regretted it, and in return Gina, who did not work, had looked after Nicky. When her own baby had arrived ten months after Nicky's birth he had been fascinated by the child, and Briony bitterly regretted that he, like her, would never know the pleasure of having brothers and sisters.

They went upstairs together, Gina pushing open the door to her flat and standing aside as a small dark-haired tornado flung himself into Briony's open arms. As she cradled the soft and infinitely precious body of her son in her arms Briony gave a tiny sigh of relief. He smelled of baby powder and clean skin, his dark, thick hair still damp from his bath, his eyes huge and reproachful as he asked where she had been.

'I've been at work, earning lots of pennies,' she told him softly.

Nicky knew that his mummy had to earn pennies, but Briony still felt an unbearable pang every time she had to tell him. She had already missed so much of his young life and he was growing up so quickly. Gina was more of a mother to him than she was.

'He's had his tea,' Gina told her with a smile. Briony thanked her without taking her eyes off her son, her expression illuminated with love and pride. The people who worked with her would never have recognised Doug's cold, withdrawn secretary in this adoring young woman. Tonight as she went over each belovedly familiar feature she found herself scrutinising them more than normal, her heart thumping betrayingly.

'Have you been good for Gina?' she asked him.

He nodded solemnly, eyes twinkling, and Briony's heart contracted on a wave of love. He had wound his way so tenaciously into her heart and life, this child whom she had borne in such pain and despair, without realising that her love for him would far outweigh the circumstances of his birth.

'Go and get your toys for Mummy,' Gina instructed him, closing the living room door behind him as he toddled off obediently. Italian parents adored their children and spoiled them lavishly, and yet they were also wise in teaching them good manners and obedience. Briony too was firm about not giving in to the impulse to over-compensate for her absences by too much indulgence, and already Nicky knew what was and was not permissible.

He was an attractive child, with soft dimples and a roguish smile, his dark curly hair making him easily mistakable for Gina's own child. Briony never made any attempt to hide her unmarried state. She was proud of her son and loved him dearly, but she also wanted him to grow up in truth.

'What's wrong?' she asked Gina anxiously as she closed the door.

'Nothing really. It was just that while we were in the Park today Nicky started asking about his father. He's very intelligent, you know, Briony. He sees that Caterina has a mummy and daddy and constantly he asks me what has happened to his daddy.' She saw the look of anguish in Briony's eyes and mistaking its cause said gently, 'Can it really be that his father does not want him? Surely. . . .'

'His father doesn't even know he exists,' Briony told her harshly, taking a deep breath. 'Oh, Gina, please don't ask me about him. Not tonight of all nights. I just couldn't bear it. . . .'

'For Nicky's sake you must,' Gina said gently. 'You cannot fob him off for ever. Soon he will be old enough for play school, and children can be so unkind. . . .'

'One-parent families are nothing unusual these days,' Briony defended, 'and surely Nicky is better off with me than with two parents who fight continuously, or worse——'

Watching her compassionately, Gina said softly, 'He is a sensitive child, and when he asks about his daddy there is such a puzzled, hurt look in his eyes that my heart fails me. Today he asked me if his daddy didn't want him.' She spread her hands wide in a gesture of dismay. 'What could I say? Fortunately I managed to distract his attention, but he is growing all the time. He is two; soon he will be three. . . . What are you going to tell him?'

'What can I tell him?' Briony asked bitterly. 'He was conceived entirely by accident, and my . . . affair with his father was long over by the time I discovered I was expecting a child.' Her lips twisted bitterly. 'How do you tell a child that his father doesn't care a row of beans for his existence, which is the truth?' They heard the door opening and Nicky ran towards them clutching a huge teddy bear and a bag of plastic bricks.

'Say goodnight to Gina,' Briony instructed him.

Later, when she was tucking him up in bed, she inspected his features carefully. He showed his fathering, this child born out of what she had thought a night of perfect love and which instead had been an act of ruthless and deliberate expediency. He had nothing of her in him, unless it was his temperament. In looks he was all Kieron; his father in exact miniature from his dark blue eyes to his thick glossy hair.

When she first discovered she was pregnant she had been out of work and depressed. She had fainted twice in one week and put it down to nervous strain until, despite the fact that she had barely been eating, she discovered that her skirt wouldn't fasten round her waist. She had known the truth then, but refused to accept it, confirmation finally coming in the shabby, impersonal interview room of a pregnancy advice bureau. They had been kind and helpful, offering to arrange for a termination of her pregnancy, despite its advanced state. They had probably considered that she wasn't capable of bringing up a child, she thought wryly. She had been practically hysterical with all that she had endured from the Press and police, and the information that she was expecting Kieron's child could have been the final straw which tipped her into insanity.

When it came to the point, though, she could not go through with it. As though bearing her child was some means of punishing herself for being so easily taken in by Kieron, she forced herself to accept it.

When he had been born, after a night of pain and anguish, she had not even wanted to look at him, but the midwife, experienced in the ways and mysteries of birth, had placed him in her arms, and from that moment she had been lost.

God had seen fit to grant her the gift of life, the midwife had said softly, and Briony had held to that thought in the long lonely months which followed.

Since then it had afforded her some slight satisfaction to know that Kieron had been deprived of this child, who must surely be the most perfect being ever created. It hadn't been easy trying to bring him up single-handed, continually torn by the desire to be with him, gloating over every tiny step forward, and the need to earn sufficient money to safeguard their future.

Until recently he had accepted quite readily the fact that he only had a 'mummy', but as Gina had said, he was quick and intelligent, and it would not be long before he was questioning why he did not have a father.

It would not make any difference, she assured herself firmly; *she* would give him everything that two parents could, and never, never would he be allowed to know how callous had been his conception.

She watched him while he slept, wondering what little-boy dreams he dreamed, her forehead puckered in a faint frown as she contemplated the future.

Briony glanced at her watch and grimaced. Nicky was being unusually fractious this morning, and she wondered if he had caught her own tense mood. He had played naughtily with his breakfast, something he never normally did, his mouth sulky and pouting when she scolded him.

'Don't go to work, Mummy,' he pleaded tearfully. 'Stay with me!'

'You know I have to go, Nicky,' she reminded him gently, 'but tomorrow's Friday, and then after that Mummy will be at home with you for two whole days. Perhaps we'll go somewhere nice, if you're a good boy for Gina.'

'Where nice?' he breathed, tears forgotten. 'To the

Zoo to see the bears?'

'Maybe. Finish your egg, there's a good boy.'

His recalcitrance had made her late, and although she ran all the way down the bottom of the avenue, she was just in time to see her bus go sailing past. Groaning, she pressed a hand to her side to stifle the aching stitch. She was going to be late, and there was nothing she could do about it, so she might as well make up her mind to accept the fact. Although she frequently worked late, she hated being late in the morning, but Doug would understand. Not that he knew about Nicky. No one at the office had the slightest inkling that she had a child, and that was the way she wanted it to stay. Employers were wary of young women without husbands and with babies to bring up, and she had always needed her job too much to risk it. Besides, she didn't want people talking about her behind her back, speculating about the identity of Nicky's father, and now with Kieron Blake working on the paper she was glad she had kept silent. He hadn't even asked her why she had changed her name, she thought bitterly—although she had not changed it entirely. Her name had been Elisabeth Briony and all she had done had been to drop her first name and change her surname for her mother's maiden name. But then no doubt he had no need to ask. He must have followed the details in the papers—and there had been plenty. He must have known the ordeal she had endured; the shock she had sustained on learning that the man she had thought of as her tender, caring lover, ready to protect her from everything, was in fact a hardbitten journalist in search of a story, and ready to do anything to get it.

It was ten past nine when she walked into her
office. She removed her jacket with a sigh.

'So. You've arrived, have you?'

She swung round, eyes widening at the silky
drawl, her heart jerking as though it were on strings.

'You're damn near ten minutes late,' Kieron
rapped out. 'Is this morning an exception, or am I to
prepare myself for your tardy arrival every day?'

He was just trying to goad her, she told herself.
After Doug's praise and recommendation he could
hardly just fire her, and so he would have to find
some other means of ridding himself of her. She
almost laughed aloud at the irony of it. He couldn't
have been very pleased to discover that the one
person in the world who knew exactly what kind of
man he was would be his new secretary.

'I'm sorry I'm late,' she apologised coldly, picking
up the post from her desk. 'I'll just go through this
and then I'll be right with you.'

He let her get to her chair before he spoke, his
voice like a whip as he drawled sarcastically,

'Hey, lady, just where the hell do you think you're
going with that stuff? Nobody puts me down like
that. And I'm perfectly capable of going through
my own mail. No doubt Doug relied heavily on you
for such assistance, but I don't need it. Get it?'

She handed him the mail with a cool, composed
smile and an expressionless,

'Yes, Mr Blake. Where is Doug, by the way?' she
enquired. It wasn't like her boss not to be in the
office early.

'Making his goodbyes, I believe,' Kieron told her
laconically. 'Today's his last day. . . .'

'Oh, but I thought. . . .' The words rose unchecked to her lips, silenced as he perched on the end of her desk and swivelled round to study her.

'You thought what? That I'd need him to nurse-maid me for longer?' He shook his head decisively. 'This kitchen only needs one cook—me. Much as I like and respect Doug I don't need him standing at my elbow overseeing everything I do. And I'm sure he would feel the same in my shoes.'

Briony knew that he would, but it didn't stop her saying acidly, 'It didn't take you very long, did it? First you try to get rid of his secretary and then you want to get rid of him.'

'Doug said to remind you that he expects you to be with the others at the pub tonight for the cele-brations,' Kieron told her casually. 'I believe your boy-friend will be there.'

It was on the tip of her tongue to tell him that she didn't have any boy-friends, and then she realised that he meant Matt.

'I shan't be going,' she said shortly. She hadn't come dressed for partying, although her slim cream skirt and pretty floral blouse were perfectly suitable for a comradely drink, and neither had she warned Gina that she would be late. She had assumed that Doug would postpone any celebrations until Friday, but she was totally unprepared for the icy disdain in Kieron's eyes as he said coldly:

'You take pleasure in spoiling other people's fun, don't you, Briony? Briony—what made you chose that name? I can see why you had to get rid of the "Beth". Far too sweet and simple for such an Amazon as you've become. What thoughts run through that cold little brain, I wonder? Can't you even permit yourself to become human for just as long as it takes to speed Doug cheerfully on his way?'

'You have no right to talk to me like this!' She was trembling with mingled fear and anger. It was as though the scales had dropped from her eyes and she was seeing him properly for the first time, not as her childish adoration had painted him. How could she ever have thought of this man as a tender lover, or a gentle protector? He was a predator; a hunter who killed and maimed, an outlaw from society's rules.

The door opened and Doug walked in, his sharp eyes going from Kieron to herself.

'How about a cup of coffee, love?' he suggested to Briony, adding to Kieron, 'Briony's a marvel. Until she came I had to make do with the canteen rubbish, but now we have properly made, freshly brewed coffee every morning. Better treatment than you got in the States, I'll bet.'

'Over there they have machines—less time-wasting. What happens if Briony is ever off? Do you use the pool, or. . . .'

Briony stiffened instinctively forcing herself not to look at him. He was trying to discover if there was any other secretary he could replace her with. Doug raised his eyebrows.

'Well, when Briony's on holiday I use one of the girls from the pool. It's not an ideal situation, but we get by. You are coming down for a drink tonight, aren't you, Briony?'

'I don't know . . . I'm not dressed. . . .'

'I wish that was true,' Doug grinned appreciatively. 'Of course you're coming. I'll go and let you two get better acquainted. Keep the coffee hot,' he added as he strode out of the room.

'Got them all going, haven't you?' Kieron commented. 'I never thought you'd turn out to be a seductress.'

She swallowed the insult, glad that she had her back to him.

'Leave that,' he instructed sharply, when she went to pick up the coffee percolator. 'We've got work to do.'

She accompanied him into his office, sitting down opposite him and angling her chair deliberately so that her legs were hidden by the desk. She didn't imagine for a moment that he would want to ogle her, but she wasn't going to give him the opportunity of suggesting that she might have wanted him to. His eyes were hard as he noted the manoeuvre, and as though in punishment he dictated at a speed far in excess of Doug's more leisurely style. Briony wasn't worried. She enjoyed taking shorthand and in other circumstances would have found his speed something of an enjoyable challenge. However, because it was him she concentrated grimly on making the neat outlines, her pencil poised for the next spate, as the ring of the phone interrupted them.

He listened in silence, and then drawled,

'Offended, my dear Gail? I'm highly flattered. It isn't every day a beautiful woman invites me out to lunch. One suit you?'

Flushing angrily at being forced to eavesdrop on his personal conversation, Briony gritted her teeth and stared coldly into space, caught off guard when he said evenly:

'Right, read that last letter back to me, will you? I've forgotton where I was.'

Briony was reasonably sure that he was lying. The letter was long and complicated, but she read through it without haste or check, her diction smooth and even. When she had finished she raised her eyes to find Kieron watching her with an exceedingly sardonic expression.

'It's almost like having my own personal computer,' he mocked cruelly. 'Don't you ever feel like coming down off your mountain and joining the rest of the human race?'

'Not as long as it includes you,' Briony retorted bitterly, paling too late as she saw his expression.

'So that's it,' he said softly, getting up from behind his desk and coming towards her. He was wearing an expensively tailored lightweight suit in dove grey, the narrow trousers moulding his thighs, and her eyes fastened helplessly on his lean hips as he came slowly towards her.

'Don't blame it all on me, Briony. You. . . .'

'I was a stupid fool,' she stormed bitterly. 'And you took full advantage of that fact, didn't you, Kieron? God, I hate you! If you burned in hell for ever more it wouldn't be enough to satisfy me!'

'Is that why you're insisting on staying here?' he grated at her. 'Are you looking for revenge? Is that how your warped little mind works?'

'I'm staying here because I need a job,' she told him coldly. 'And I don't think the Board would be very impressed with their new editor if I told them why he was so anxious to get rid of me. Rival papers would love it, though, I'm sure. Selling sensation life stories seems to be all the rage these days. I wonder how much my exposé would be worth?'

'It works both ways,' he retorted softly. 'By working for me, you're putting yourself within my power, and after what you've just admitted, doesn't that thought frighten you?'

'Not in the least,' Briony lied bravely. 'You've already done your worst. Anything else could only be an anticlimax.'

He gave her so much work that it was lunchtime before she could ring Gina to warn her that she might be late.

The Italian girl was delighted to hear that she was going out. 'You took my warning about Nicky to heart, eh?' she teased. 'I wish you luck in your search for a papa for him.'

Briony had worked through her lunch-hour and expecting that Kieron would be detained by Gail had not thought to close her office door when she made her call. The result was that he walked in when she was right in the middle of it, and Gina was describing Nicky's newest trick.

'Personal call?' Kieron said sardonically when she had finished. 'First time I've seen a spark of life in you since I got here. Does Matt know about him?'

'My private affairs are my own,' Briony retorted, colour scorching her skin as she realised the inference he had drawn from her words. Of course he would think she meant love affairs. She turned her back on him, searching through the files for an article she needed. When she straightened up Kieron was standing right behind her. She could smell the faint tang of his aftershave. His skin was firm and tanned, the blue eyes framed with ridiculously thick dark lashes. Just like Nicky's. Her heart pounded, and she bent down to close the cupboard drawer, trying to conceal her reaction. Kieron frowned suddenly.

'You still use the same perfume.'

Anger flooded her at his cruelty.

'I'm surprised you remembered,' she said bitterly. 'But then reporters are trained to remember every small detail, however minor, aren't they? That's how you managed to piece together your scoop, wasn't it? How boring it must have been for you to have to search through all the dross of my confidences for those precious nuggets! But well worth it in the end. As Gail said, the story made you famous overnight. As it did me, although in my case the word was "infamous". I'm surprised you didn't tell them all yesterday exactly who I was. Or can it be that you actually felt ashamed of admitting exactly how you got your story?'

'You weren't exactly unwilling,' he reminded her harshly.

'I wasn't unwilling to let you make love to me, but I wasn't given the opportunity to state my views on how you intended to use my confidences, was I? I wish I could think that having me working for you would put you through hell, Kieron, but we both know that you don't have that much compunction, don't we?'

He reached for her, but she was ready for him, sliding behind her desk and sitting down. Anger blazed in his eyes, his skin stretched tautly across the bones of his face. He had removed his jacket and his thin silk shirt showed the smoothly muscled wall of his chest with its covering of dark hair. With a sense of shock she realised that he was intensely male; something she had never fully appreciated before. Because he had hidden that side of himself from her? Of course he had never been attracted to her. He was the sort of man who had women coming out of his ears. How he must have laughed at her naïveté!

By five o'clock her desk was clear, but her head was pounding and all she wanted to do was to go home and go to bed. The heat in the city was oppressive, beating up off the pavements and clogging the air to mingle chokingly with the petrol fumes.

When she went down to the cloakroom to freshen up several of the other girls were already there.

'What a waste!' a giggly blonde from Fashion moaned to her friend. They were bent over one of the basins and neither of them had seen Briony come in. 'That gorgeous hunk of male and Ice-Cold Winters! I bet she wouldn't know what to do with a real man. Look at that wet Matt she goes about with!'

Someone kicked her on the ankle and she turned round complaining, her mouth dropping open when she saw Briony. For a moment Briony had a savage longing to tell her that she knew exactly what to do with a man like Kieron Blake, but she suppressed it, pretending she had heard nothing, which was stupid because the girl had a particularly shrill voice.

'Ice-Cold Winters.' Was that what they called her? She grimaced and then shrugged dismissively. What did it matter after all?

CHAPTER THREE

THE others were all gathered in the pub when Briony
got there. Doug greeted her cheerfully, throwing his
arm round her shoulders and insisting on buying her
what she suspected was a highly lethal drink. She
sipped it slowly, grimacing a little as the raw spirit
hit her throat. The paper's staff were well known in
the small pub and a buffet meal had been organised.
Briony left Doug chatting to some colleagues and
went to fill her plate, glancing discreetly at her
watch. At eight o'clock she would make her excuses
and leave. She knew from past experience that a
hard core of staff would remain as long as the bar
stayed open, but she had told Gina to expect her
about nine. She hated missing Nicky's bedtime.
Bathing him and tucking him up in bed was
something she looked forward to all day.

Matt materialised at her side while she was standing by the buffet table. His face was pale and he was
already a little unsteady on his feet.

'Got to talk to you,' he muttered. 'Let's go and sit
down.'

Briony frowned. Matt had too much to drink, and
it showed in his faintly slurred speech and dull eyes.
Rather than create a scene she let him lead her to a
small table, unobtrusively pushing her plate of food
in front of him, guessing that he had had nothing to
eat.

Gail was standing in front of them and Briony's

46

heart sank when she saw Kieron come towards her, hoping that he would not see them sitting behind his companion.

'It's Mary,' Matt confided unsteadily. 'She wants to come back to me. Her mother rang me this morning. Oh God, Briony, I just can't believe it!' His voice broke and Briony was dismayed to see that there were tears in his eyes. It struck her that his wife was far more fortunate than she deserved, and that it might do the marriage good were Matt not to appear too over-eager to take her back.

'What did you say?' she asked him cautiously. A tiny voice was warning her that it would be imprudent to embroil herself in Matt's private life, and that once she did, she would be a prop that he would lean on for ever more.

'I didn't say anything,' he confessed.

'Then if you take my advice you won't,' Briony told him crisply. 'At least not for a while.'

Matt was staring at her open-mouthed, but it was the open disdain in another pair of eyes, steel-blue with contempt, that made her flush. No one else had witnessed the small exchange. Kieron glanced away almost immediately, and Briony frowned, shrugging aside her momentary reaction, to concentrate on Matt.

'I'm sure Mary will appreciate you far more if you don't go running back to her straight away, Matt, but the decision must be yours. Look, I must go and say goodbye to Doug, and then I'm leaving.'

'Stay a bit longer, and I'll give you a lift home,' Matt urged. 'I've got the car.'

'No, really, I can't,' she told him, standing up to look for Doug.

He greeted her with a rueful smile.

'Don't tell me you're running off already?'

'Got to, I'm afraid,' she said casually. Gail and Kieron had joined the group round the bar, and she felt herself colour as Gail drawled in cool amusement:

'A boy-friend? You do surprise me! Who is he? Or can we guess?'

She was looking at Matt as she spoke, her eyes openly deriding, and Briony squashed an impulse to tell her the truth.

'How about a kiss for good luck?' Doug suggested. He looked at her like a playful puppy, and Briony knew that if she refused he would be hurt. Leaning forward, she kissed him lightly on the cheek, while several of the others cheered. As though he knew how much the gesture had cost her Doug whispered, 'Thanks, honey. Take it easy with Kieron, he's not me, you know.'

'Unfortunately.' The word was out before she could stop it, but before Doug could make any comment Matt had lurched up to them, his expression belligerent as he threw his arm round Briony.

'Briony's with me,' he told the older man. 'I'm taking you home—aren't I, Briony?'

Too furious to speak, Briony pulled away, but Matt refused to let her go. The alcohol he had consumed seemed to have wrought a sea-change to his character, and far from being embarrassed by his behaviour he seemed inclined to become even more possessive.

'I think you've had a little too much to drink, old man,' Kieron interrupted calmly, his hand going out to restrain him. Matt shook him off, and for a moment Briony felt fear crawling along her spine as she saw the look in Kieron's eyes. It vanished almost instantly, to be replaced with one of cool contempt.

'Got to take Briony home,' Matt muttered, subsiding a little as though even his muddled brain had perceived the danger.

'I'll take her home. You're in no fit state to drive,' Kieron told him in clipped accents. 'In fact I think we'd better have your car keys, unless of course you were planning on staying with Briony overnight.'

There was an electric silence when Briony directed a freezing glare at Kieron and the others shuffled uncomfortably, avoiding her eyes.

'No?' Kieron drawled. 'Hardly surprising. Give me your keys and Gail here will make sure you get home safely—won't you, Gail?'

The blonde looked surprised and slightly chagrined, and Briony wondered how Kieron knew that Gail and Matt lived quite close to one another. Unless perhaps Gail had told him? It was plain from the other girl's expression that she had expected to be the one going home with Kieron, and the look she directed at Briony was openly hostile.

'I don't need anyone to take me home,' Briony announced firmly. 'I'm perfectly capable of taking myself. In fact I must leave now or I'll miss my bus.'

'You're not walking through the streets alone at this time of night,' Kieron told her in clipped accents, his fingers closing about her arm and forestalling her flight. It was hot in the pub and he had discarded his jacket, his tie pulled loosely away from his shirt collar, which was unbuttoned to reveal the tanned skin of his throat.

'This isn't New York,' Briony countered, but Doug

was frowning slightly.

'He's right, you know, Briony,' he told her. 'It isn't wise to walk alone in London at night.'

It seemed as though they had all entered into a conspiracy against her, one of the younger reporters recounting with obvious relish stories of muggings—and worse. Even allowing for certain embellishments they did not make pleasant hearing, and Briony felt the gooseflesh prickle along her arms as she contemplated the long walk to her bus stop. Urban violence was a fact of life and it would be foolish to ignore it. Even Matt seemed to accept that Kieron was going to take her home, and sulkily handed his keys over to Gail.

Kieron did not release his grip of her arm, and as they made their final goodbyes she hissed at him, 'There's really no need. You don't even know where I live. I could be taking you miles out of your way.'

'I know all right,' he told her grimly. 'I've been through all the staff files—and now unless you really want to see me lose my temper, just shut up, will you?'

His car wasn't parked very far away, but Kieron retained his hold of her arm, forcing her to try to match her small paces to his longer ones as they walked along the pavement. Briony glimpsed their reflection in a store window. To an onlooker their pose represented that of close friends—or lovers. She pulled away, shivering suddenly, although the evening was quite mild. How often in the past had they walked together like this? But then she had had no thought in her head but the sheer thrilling pleasure of Kieron's proximity.

She was so deep in thought that she didn't realise

at first that Kieron had stopped next to a long, sleek, pale grey car, which looked both fast and dangerous.

'Get in,' he instructed her, unlocking the passenger door and standing over her while she did to.

She sank into the luxurious hide upholstery, unwillingly impressed by the opulence of the vehicle. When Kieron got in beside her and slammed his door she moved instinctively farther towards hers, oppressed by the unwanted intimacy the narrow confines of the car forced upon her.

When Kieron turned towards her, she flinched, her eyes wide and dark, colour running up angrily under her skin as he reached casually for the seat belt and held it up mockingly in front of her.

'What did you think I was going to do? Give way to the violent passion of my feelings and make love to you?'

'Don't be so ridiculous!' She was thankful that long habit gave her the ability to inject ice into her voice, her eyes staring rigidly ahead of her as Kieron snapped the seat belt into its holder. He hadn't touched her, and yet for a moment she had been intensely aware of him in a way that brought unwanted memories crowding back. Inside she was trembling with reaction and fear, but she willed herself not to betray it, saying nothing as Kieron started the car. It moved off with a powerful, throaty roar, Briony sitting silent at his side.

He glanced at her once or twice, but when she refused to look back he switched on the cassette player, inserting a tape.

The voice of Rita Coolidge filled the car. She was singing something haunting and sad about parting lovers, and Briony felt the skin of her scalp prickle warningly.

'Still sulking because I broke up your "romance"? Kieron drawled. 'There's no need for me to ask if you know that he's married already, of course. Do you love him?'

The question caught her off guard, her eyes green and angry as she glared at him.

'That's no business of yours!'

'Sure it is. You're both on my staff. Love affairs in the office play havoc with performance.'

'And you're concerned that my "affair" with Matt might affect my work?' she said sweetly. 'Don't worry—it won't.'

'I'll bet,' Kieron drawled succinctly. 'He doesn't look as though he's got what it takes to keep one woman satisfied, never mind two.'

His sheer audacity all but took her breath away, and she turned on him angrily, her determination not to speak to him forgotten.

'How I feel about Matt has nothing to do with you. And I don't want to talk about it. Just drop me here, and I'll make the rest of the way alone.'

She reached angrily for the door handle, and Kieron swore viciously, the car screeching to a halt. And then he was reaching for her, his face white with fury, his eyes murderous with rage.

He shook her like a rag doll.

'Don't you ever try anything like that again, you silly little bitch! What the hell were you going to do? Fling yourself out on to the road? We were doing forty miles an hour back there, in case it had escaped your notice. Do you know what a road surface could do to your skin at that speed? It would have been ripped to ribbons!'

'Stop it!' Briony was feeling faintly sick, her head throbbing painfully with shock and fright. She had never really intended to open the car door; he had just made her so angry that she had reached for it automatically.

He let her go with a smothered imprecation, his hands tightening on the steering wheel and a white line of rage round his mouth. Briony glanced covertly at him. For a moment in his arms she had been filled with a wild, fierce satisfaction as she felt his anger beat up to meet her own, but now it was gone, her imagination painting pictures of what would have happened to her if she had succeeded in opening the door.

Kieron seemed to be simply staring into space, and she wondered what thoughts were running through his mind. In one short day he had made his presence felt on the paper, and people were already beginning to speak of him with respect. He had intense pride and resilience, and it must go against the grain to have her constantly under his nose—a reminder of what he had done to her. Or perhaps it didn't bother him. Perhaps he was ruthless enough to pretend it had never happened.

He started the car again without speaking. There was a faint clicking noise and when Briony looked puzzled, he explained coldly, 'An automatic locking device for the doors. If you insist on behaving like a child then you deserve to be treated like one—or would it give you some sort of twisted satisfaction to kill yourself in my presence?'

Her hands, which were lying in her lap, itched to slap his face, but she contented herself with a cold stare, her eyes the colour of sea in winter.

Kieron only had to ask her the way once, when they turned off the main road into her avenue, and as the grey car slid to a halt in front of the house, she was glad that it was dark and that Gina and Paolo could not witness her arrival—or her companion.

She turned to open her door the moment the car stopped, forgetting that it was locked.

Kieron eyed her sardonically.

'Oh no, you don't,' he said softly. 'We've got things to talk about, you and I. Did you really think you could get away with the sort of treatment you've been dishing out? I'm not Matt, Briony.'

'No, I know,' she replied coldly. 'I know exactly what type of man you are, Kieron. Ruthless, deceitful, completely without compassion or compunction. . . . Do I have to go on? Oh, don't worry,' she added icily when he didn't speak, 'you won't lose your reputation. The big clever reporter who got a front page scoop, and turned his back on the poor little fool who give it to him, leaving her to face the wolves!'

He reached across the seat, his fingers biting into her arms. 'It wasn't like that,' he ground out. 'I. . . . Oh, what the hell!' he pushed her away from him, his expression unfathomable. 'Don't put all the blame on me, Briony. You did your bit, although you might choose to forget it now. It wasn't all one-sided.'

'Let me out of this car,' Briony demanded tensely. 'I think you're the most contemptible person I've ever met! Oh, God, don't touch me!' she moaned frantically, seeking to avoid the hard strength of his hands as he all but yanked her out of her seat, hauling her against him and keeping her a prisoner there while her eyes spat hatred and defiance.

'Go on, hit me,' he goaded softly, watching the hurried rise and fall of her breasts beneath the thin blouse. She twisted desperately to free herself, but her agitated movements merely brought her closer to the unwanted intimacy of his body, as Kieron grasped both her wrists in one hand and pulled her on to his knee.

'I hate you!' Tears threatened and she willed them not to fall. Her heart was hammering anxiously, every muscle tensed against him, fear rising up inside her like a tidal wave. Oh, God, she didn't want him to touch her. She couldn't bear it. No one had touched her since he left, and she sometimes thought that if they did she might actually be sick, so strong was her fear that the feelings she had deliberately dammed up inside herself might burst their banks and sweep her into the same sort of dangerous waters she had once experienced with Kieron. If one man skilled in physical pleasure could arouse her so easily, then might not others? She had refused to accept that it was her own overwhelming love for Kieron which had lowered her guard. Love did not exist, it was merely a euphemism for sex which men used to coax women into submitting to them.

'Hate is akin to love, so they say,' Kieron mocked.

'Love!' Her body stiffened, her voice high and strained. 'The mere thought of having you near me makes me feel physically sick!' she flung at him.

'Does it now?'

The silky, dangerous tone set her nerve ends quivering with fear. She tensed automatically, turning away as his head descended, but his free hand forced it back again, his fingers tightening painfully in her hair to keep her head still as his mouth covered hers, with hard, angry pressure.

She fought desperately against the dominance of his kiss, her mouth tightly closed, her eyes spitting fury into the glittering darkness of his. When his hand released her head, she thought she had won and struggled triumphantly to sit up, but the pressure of his body kept her wedged against the door, and then his hand swept down her body, ruthlessly deepening the opening of her blouse, his fingers almost brutal as they closed over her breast.

Her lips parted on a gasp, his victory instantly reinforced by the hardness of his mouth as it punished her earlier defiance. If she had feared that the embrace might evoke unbearable memories, she need not have done. It was no coaxing, gentle caress, designed to soothe the fears of a young innocent girl, but a punishment, to humiliate and degrade, the tender inner flesh of her lips ground mercilessly against her teeth until it was torn and sore.

His touch was an insulting parody of what a lover's should be, and after the first initial shock, her flesh cringed beneath his hand. She was entirely at his mercy, and anger gave way to overwhelming fear as she realised the depth of the rage which gripped him.

Panic made her struggle frantically, her rebellion ruthlessly subdued as Kieron reinforced his mastery. The buttons on her blouse had given way beneath his attack, the soft curve of her breast clearly visible, and she closed her eyes in horror as she felt Kieron move, anticipating his intention. She felt his breath against her skin, a cold, icy mist, slowly creeping over her as she tried feebly to push him away, her eyes dilating with fear. Her soft moan halted him, and the next moment she was sitting upright in her own seat, Kieron's voice terse as he said acidly, 'There's no need to faint. You're not some fragile Victorian heroine enduring the unwanted attentions of a wicked Sir Jasper. My God, though, it's true what they say. You're as cold as ice, aren't you?'

'I'm what you made me!' Briony hurled at him through numb lips. 'What did you expect? That I would fall into your arms with cries of rapture? Let me out of here!' Her voice shook and a dreadful inertia seemed to spread through her. They had been outside the house for less than fifteen minutes, but it seemed like a lifetime. This time when she reached for the handle, the door swung open instantly, and then she was out on the pavement, breathing in the cool, clear air, her legs feeling as though they were stuffed with cotton wool.

She couldn't face Gina and Paolo. Unlocking the door to her own flat, she went into her bedroom, staring blindly at her reflection in the mirror. Her hair was ruffled, her mouth swollen and bruised. There were the beginnings of faint marks against the flesh of her breast, and shuddering with disgust she ripped off her blouse and bra, rolling them up into a ball and throwing them into the wastepaper bin. Never mind the fact that both were comparatively new, she could not bear to have either of them close to her skin again.

She showered in icy water, the blood beating up painfully under her skin. She felt sick and dizzy and wanted to lie down, but to do so would mean giving

in to the fear Kieron had ignited, so she forced herself
to dress again, brushing her hair and securing it with
an elastic band, before going upstairs to collect
Nicky.

Gina glanced at her rather speculatively when she
opened the door, and Briony knew that despite her
attempts to disguise it, the other girl had noticed her
bruised mouth, although she was too tactful to
comment.

'I'm sorry I'm a bit late,' she apologised. 'Is
everything okay?'

'Fine. Are you all right?' Gina asked bluntly. 'You
don't look well.'

'I've got a headache.' It was true. Her head was
pounding and she was shivering even though it
wasn't really cold.

Paolo insisted on carrying Nicky downstairs for
her, and he barely stirred. Lucky Nicky, Briony
thought enviously. If only her life was as simple and
uncomplicated as his!

Nicky was crying, the thin sound punctured her
nightmare. She wanted to go to him, but she couldn't
move. Something was holding her back, preventing
her from reaching her son. She clawed desperately
to be free, calling to Nicky to wait for her, but then
he turned round and his face was Kieron's, cold and
hatefully mocking.

'No . . .!' The sound was torn from her throat,
and she opened her eyes groggily, the bedroom spun
round, and waves of nausea rushed over her as she
tried to lift her head from the pillow.

Migraine! She slumped back, trying to force her
mind to concentrate on where she had put her pills.

It was ages since she had last had an attack, and she had no need to ask what had caused this one.

Nicky had recently been promoted from his cot to his own small bed, and she could hear him padding about in his own room. She glanced at the alarm clock, knowing that it would be impossible for her to go to work. Her attacks, although rare, were unbelievably violent. Sickness and temporary paralysis were merely two of the symptoms she had suffered in the past, and she reached for the phone intending to call the paper. As she did so, she heard Gina's key turn in her front door, and the Italian girl hurried into the bedroom, her expression concerned.

'So you are ill—I thought you must be. What is it?'

'Migraine,' Briony croaked. 'I was just trying to ring the office.'

'Leave all that to me,' Gina said firmly. 'Now where are your pills? Would you like a drink?'

Before she went she insisted on straightening Briony's bed and bringing her a mug of tea. Nicky toddled in to look at her with huge, grave eyes, his voice sympathetic as he murmured, 'Mummy got bad headache?'

It was bliss to feel sleep steal over her as the pills began to take effect. As Briony knew from past experience, the only cure for such an attack was sleep. By tomorrow she could well be fully recovered, although a little weak, and her last conscious thought was that now Kieron would have an opportunity to try out her substitute.

It was evening before she woke up, and she knew the moment she opened her eyes that the pain had gone. As always after such an attack her body felt terribly weak, and it seemed to take twice as long as usual to go through the motions of washing and dressing.

When she knocked on Gina's door, Nicky greeted her joyfully, his 'Mummy better?' making her flesh melt with love.

Gina insisted on her eating with them, announcing that Briony was far from well enough to prepare a meal.

'You do too much,' she scolded. 'And this weather we've been having doesn't help.'

It had been unusually warm, but Briony knew that the close atmosphere was not really responsible for her illness. Gina's little girl was just starting to talk, with Nicky acting importantly as interpreter. She was a lovely child, with huge pansy brown eyes and thick lustrous curls, and watching her and Nicky together, Briony felt another pang of guilt that Nicky was an only child. He was already so protective and sweet with Caterina, and she, knowing female that she was, played up to him with coy smiles and flashing dimples.

Gina and Paolo were good company. They were really her only close friends. After her experiences with the Press Briony had been wary of confiding in anyone. She had returned once to the village where she had been brought up, but the story had spread like wildfire and she had been treated like an outcast. Sir Arthur had been very well thought of locally, although people didn't have much time for his son, and Briony had left, vowing that she would never return.

'Oh, by the way, I spoke to your boss,' Gina announced carelessly, unaware of the effect of her words. 'He was most concerned when I told him you were ill.'

'You didn't mention Nicky?'

Gina looked puzzled. 'No.'

Briony sagged in relief, forcing a smile. 'It's just that the people at work don't know about him. . . .'

Although Gina accepted the explanation, Briony sensed that she was curious and prayed that her friend would never have occasion to set eyes upon Kieron.

Nicky chattered unceasingly as she got him ready for bed. He paused in the middle of telling her how brave he had been when Paolo threw him up in the air, studying her reproachfully.

'Why haven't I got a daddy?' he asked tremulously.

'You've got me,' Briony said casually. 'Aren't I enough?' She knew she wasn't being fair, but Nicky was still far too young to appreciate the complexities of adult relationships.

'I want a daddy as well,' he insisted stubbornly, refusing to let her hug him. 'You can't play with me properly like a daddy can.'

He didn't mean to be hurtful, Briony reminded herself as tears blurred his small soapy body. It was easy to distract his attention from 'daddies' to bears as she reminded him that she was taking him to the Zoo, but as she read his bedtime story, she wondered wryly why the writers of children's stories always assumed that their readers' worlds encompassed two solid, dependable parents with neatly outlined roles in life.

Tonight she had managed to sidestep his questions, but she could not do so for ever, and for the first

time it struck her that her son might eventually grow
to resent her for what in his childish eyes might seem
to be her deliberate denial of his father. The injustice
of the thought brought fresh tears. If Nicky was adult
she could explain to him properly, but by the time
he was it would be too late.

CHAPTER FOUR

THE good weather held, and on Saturday morning
Briony dressed Nicky in the beautiful Italian wool-
lens Gina's mother had sent him for Christmas. The
jumper and little trousers had been a little on the
large side at the time but now fitted him perfectly,
and her heart swelled with maternal pride as they
set off hand in hand.

Paolo worked for an uncle who ran a wine im-
porting business in London, and as he had to be in
the office on Saturdays, he offered to give them a
lift.

Riding in a car was a treat for Nicky, and he
chattered constantly, drawing Briony's attention to
wondrous new sights.

The Zoo was crowded, but with the morning
stretching ahead of them there was no need to rush.
Briony had brought Nicky's pushchair for when he
grew tired. It was only when she saw other children
that she appreciated how well behaved her own son
was. He stared at the animals in awed delight, his
concentration drawing admiring smiles from other
adults. Holding his hand and feeling his solid body

pressed against her in trust and love, Briony felt almost overwhelmed with emotion.

Before they began the long trudge home she bought him an icecream, mopping up the drips and spills as he licked it enthusiastically.

As she had expected, he was tired when they got off the bus. He had gone off to sleep in her arms, and as she put him in his pushchair he opened his eyes drowsily to smile at her.

The day had turned unseasonally hot and sticky. Gina had gone to spend the afternoon with some friends who lived on the other side of London, and when she had put Nicky down for his nap Briony changed into an emerald green and white striped bikini and went to lie out on the lawn.

Her book failed to hold her attention and gradually her eyes closed and her body relaxed into the rug, the warmth of the sun beating into her.

She woke up with a start, conscious that she was no longer alone, her mind still fuzzy with sleep.

'Gina?'

'I hope not,' a cool, male voice drawled laconically, its owner coming to stand over her, his eyes appraising her curves beneath their flimsy covering.

'Kieron!' His name was a shocked whisper, her eyes clouding over as she tried to comprehend what he was doing in her garden. He was dressed casually in cream jeans and a thin cotton shirt open to the waist, a pair of tinted sunglasses in one hand.

'You left this in my car,' he announced, producing a thin lipstick case. 'It must have rolled out of your handbag.'

His eyes were still on her body and she forced herself not to move. Since Nicky's birth her breasts had become slightly fuller, but her waist and hips were still as slender as ever, her skin smooth and firm.

'You could have kept it until Monday,' she said in a shaken voice. 'Or are you just checking up on me? Making sure my migraine wasn't just an excuse not to come to work?'

As she spoke her eyes went instinctively to Nicky's bedroom window which overlooked the garden, and her voice automatically lowered. She daren't think about what might happen if the little boy woke up and saw them.

'Don't be stupid,' Kieron said in clipped accents. His gaze had shifted to her lips, still sore and swollen, and as Briony moved uncomfortably under his look she realised that he had suddenly gone pale, his eyes fixed on the creamy swell of her breast. Her bikini top was brief and revealing, the marks of his fingers plainly discernible against her pale flesh.

'Did I do that?' he demanded tersely.

Anger blazed briefly.

'Are you in any doubt? Do you think I enjoy being mauled about like that? Encourage it even?'

'Well, if you do, you can't get much satisfaction out of Matt,' he said cruelly. 'Adoring reverence is more his style.'

'Perhaps I find that a pleasant change.'

He reached for her before she could stop him, grasping her wrists and pulling her to her feet.

'Well now, let's just put that to the test, shall we?' he began pleasantly.

Her heart thundered against her flesh, the tip of her tongue moistening the lips nervously, a sensation close to terror shivering across her skin.

His hands left her wrists and slid gently round her waist, his eyes holding her captive like a fly in amber. The creaking of the gate freed her. Gina and Paolo were standing there staring in astonishment, and Briony's heart sank. One look at Gina's face was enough to tell her that her friend had guessed the truth.

She introduced them to Kieron curtly, her eyes darkening with pain when he bent to pick up Caterina, who was gazing at him in wonder.

She gurgled something approving, her tiny hands fastening on to his shirt, and Briony was unaware of the anguish in her eyes, until Gina touched her lightly on the arm, jolting her into awareness.

'I just dropped by to return Briony's lipstick' Kieron explained. 'She dropped it in my car the other night. I was hoping to be offered a cold drink,' he added tauntingly, 'but somehow we never got round to it.'

He was making his meaning plain, but there was no way she could invite him into her flat, Briony thought on a wave of fresh anxiety.

Gina came to her rescue.

'I made some fresh lemonade before we went out. Why don't we all go upstairs and have some?'

'I'll put a wrap on first,' Briony muttered, anxious to escape and check up on Nicky.

Fortunately he was still asleep. She dropped a light kiss on his nose as she changed into a cotton dress, wondering feverishly how quickly she could get rid of Kieron.

He and Paolo were talking about cars when she went upstairs. She was thirsty herself and Gina's lemonade was coolly refreshing. Gina started to tell her about their afternoon, when Caterina who had been playing contentedly on the floor with her toys suddenly electrified Briony by looking up at Kieron and saying quite clearly, 'Nicky'. It was her first proper word and she sat back looking very pleased with herself at having silenced so many grown-ups. Paolo was the first to recover, swinging her up into his arms and tickling her until the flat rang with her giggles.

'Who's Nicky?' Kieron asked in amusement. 'He seems to have had a profound effect on your daughter.'

'Oh, he's just a little boy she plays with,' Gina said hurriedly. 'She isn't talking properly yet. All men are "Nicky" to her at the moment,' she improvised wildly.

Briony couldn't have said a word to save her life. After that first awful moment when her eyes had flown automatically to Kieron's face she had been incapable of saying anything. If Nicky himself had suddenly appeared in the room and claimed Kieron as his father she couldn't have been more shocked.

Kieron left shortly afterwards, Paolo going with him to inspect his car. When they had gone Briony remained standing by the window staring into the garden.

'He is Nicky's father, isn't he?' Gina said softly.

It was pointless lying.

'Does he know?' Gina answered her own question. 'Of course not. But you introduced him to us as your boss?'

'It's a long story,' Briony said dryly. These people were her closest friends, and yet even to them she felt she could not confide the whole truth. Once one's ability to trust had been destroyed, nothing could restore it, she reflected unhappily, making her escape by reminding Gina that Nicky would be waking up.

'Thank goodness he didn't wake up earlier,' she added on a shudder.

'Perhaps it would have been better if he had done,' Gina said softly. 'He needs his father, Briony.'

It was no longer 'a' father, but 'his' father, Briony noted bitterly as she left.

That was the third letter she had had to re-type this morning, Briony thought tiredly as she pulled it out of her machine.

Kieron was in a savagely critical mood, which seemed to intensify with every passing day. He kept her working late almost every night and if was often way past Nicky's bedtime when she got home. She had been scouring the papers for another job, but there had been nothing. Hardly a day went by without Kieron making some caustic comment about her relationship with Matt. He had found Matt in her office one lunchtime, bursting in on them in a furious temper and demanding that Matt left her alone to get on with her work. It had been on the tip of her tongue to remind him that it was her lunch hour, but the atmosphere between them was so tensely inflammable that she had thought better of it. Time enough to tell him what she thought of him, if and when she got another job.

At the moment he was absent from the office. There had been a question of libel over an article they had printed—the nightmare of every editor, and he was down with the sub-editor of Features talking about it. The heat which seemed to hang over the city in a pall, combined with the long hours she was working, was leaving Briony feeling limp and drained. Gina complained that she did not eat properly, and Briony knew that her accusations were well founded. Since Kieron had arrived her appetite had diminished, and besides, with all the work she had to do, there simply wasn't time to eat. It had occurred to her that he was deliberately driving her hard, hoping that she would break, and this knowledge only strengthened her resolve not to give in.

The phone rang and she reached for it listlessly, her face paling as she heard Paolo's anxious voice. At first she didn't understand what he was trying to tell her, and then when she did, she dropped the receiver with a low moan, covering her face with trembling hands, trying to comprehend what had happened. The outer office door suddenly swung open and Kieron strode in, his eyes fastening on her shocked face and the dangling receiver.

'What the hell's going on?' he bit out, reaching for the phone.

Briony snatched feverishly for her handbag, getting unsteadily to her feet.

'I've got to go out. . . .' She was trembling with pain and fright, her eyes cloudy and vague, unaware of who was with her or even where she was.

'Sit down,' Kieron commanded curtly, pushing her back into her chair, but she struggled to sit up, her face white and drawn.

'I've got to go,' she said unsteadily. 'Nicky needs me,' and to her horror tears filled her eyes and rolled down her cheeks. The receiver was emitting anxious noises and Kieron spoke into it, frowning heavily.

'Blake here,' he said tersely. 'What. . . . Paolo?'

He stared at Briony, obviously listening intently. 'Okay, leave everything to me,' he said coolly. 'Which hospital?'

'So Nicky's your son?' he said grimly when he had replaced the receiver. 'God, no wonder you didn't want Matt to go back to his wife! Why the hell doesn't he stop shilly-shallying and make up his mind which one of you he wants?'

Briony barely heard him. Since Paolo had told her that Nicky was in hospital there hadn't been room for anything but her son in her mind. She had always known something like this would happen, she thought in anguish, unable to bear the thought of Nicky, ill and in pain and crying for her.

'I must go,' she muttered, pushing past Kieron.

'Just like that?'

She stared at him, his features slowly coming into focus. Like someone in a dream she said slowly, 'I've done your letters.'

'To hell with the letters!' Kieron swore viciously. 'Have you rung for a taxi?'

She shook her head and he swore again, picking up the phone and dialling a number forcefully. He said something into the receiver and then hung up, grasping Briony's arm.

'My car's outside. Come on.'

'I don't want you.'

She spoke the words from a mind cloudy with pain, pulling back as he ushered her through the door.

'Don't be so damned stupid,' Kieron said curtly. 'Your child's in hospital. All that matters is that you get to him as quickly as possible—or would you prefer me to send for Matt?'

When she said nothing he bundled her out of the room impatiently, stopping at the reception desk to say that he was going out.

In the shock of hearing that Nicky had had an accident, Briony hadn't even asked Paolo which hospital he was in, and in some distant way she felt grateful for the speed with which Kieron negotiated the traffic, without bothering her with questions.

It was only when they pulled up outside the hospital that he spoke, his voice terse and clipped.

'I take it no one at the paper knows about this child? God, you must think a hell of a lot about Matt to keep something like this secret! You can't believe he really cares about you? He's given you a child and still he doesn't divorce his wife. What are you hoping for?'

Tears welled and trickled down her cheeks. Like a child she allowed Kieron to help her out of the car, her eyes wide and blank as she followed him into Casualty.

Gina was waiting for her, her face pale and shocked.

'It was the apple tree,' she explained in anguish. 'I only left him for a moment to pay the milkman and when I got back he was lying on the ground. He's broken his arm, they think.'

It was Kieron who reassured her that the accident could have happened to the most conscientious parent.

'You can't watch them every moment of the time.'

Gina had left Caterina with a neighbour, and glanced uncertainly at Briony as though uncertain who needed her most. Kieron set her mind at rest.

'I'll stay with Briony,' he told her. 'You get back to your baby.'

The waiting room was empty and Briony stared at the painted walls, trying to subdue her rising hysteria. Somewhere out there was Nicky. She looked wildly at the door, half rising to go to it when it opened and a round-faced nurse appeared.

'Mrs Winters?' she said with a smile. 'Your little boy's fine. It's a simple, clean break and the doctor has set it for him. We're giving him a tetanus injection, just to be on the safe side. If you and your husband would like to follow me.'

Her words jolted Briony out of her nightmare. She opened her mouth to correct the girl, but she was already hurrying away. She paused once, waiting for them to catch up with her, her eyes appreciative as she looked at Kieron.

'My, your son is like you, isn't he?' she commented. 'And such a brave little scrap. He never cried once.'

Briony stopped dead, the breath leaving her lungs on a wave of panic, but a grim hand in the small of her back forced her forwards, her face pale beneath the corridor lights.

Nicky was in the children's ward, sitting on a small bed, and his face lit up the moment he saw Briony.

'I felled off the tree,' he told her importantly, 'and now my arm is being mended.'

It was obvious that he at least was none the worse for his ordeal, but Briony badly needed the reassurance of feeling his small body in her arms. He wriggled impatiently when she hugged him, his eyes sliding past her to Kieron.

'Who's that man?' he demanded warily.

Kieron was staring at Nicky in total disbelief and shocked comprehension. There would be no more comments about Matt fathering her child, Briony knew.

She ignored Nicky's question. 'Can I take him home?' she asked the nurse.

'Of course. The doctor will want to have a word with you about the plaster and so on. He's got a rather unusual blood group, did you know?'

Briony had known, and suspected that it had come down to him from his father, a suspicion which Kieron's expression confirmed.

The nurse went to attend to a crying child, and they were alone by Nicky's bed.

'God, why didn't you tell me?' Kieron swore bitterly. 'My child, and you keep it from me!'

'He's not. . . .' Briony began, but the look on Kieron's face quelled her.

'Don't lie to me,' he demanded harshly. 'That's my child and you damned well know it. We've got things to talk about, you and I. You're not simply going to walk away from this, Briony.'

The doctor's arrival halted their conversation. It galled Briony that he should so constantly address his remarks to Kieron instead of herself. In view of the likeness between father and son it would have been pointless to deny their relationship, she realised, but she could not help reflecting bitterly on the unkind twist of fate that had brought Kieron into her office just when she was at her most vulnerable. The moment Paolo had told her that Nicky had had an accident she had simply ceased to register anything else, even the fact that she had dropped the receiver in the middle of his explanation. It was ironic to think that if it had not been for that simple mistake Kieron would never have known about his child.

The doctor had finished and Briony bent to pick up Nicky.

'I'll carry him,' Kieron announced firmly. 'He's too heavy for you.'

'No!'

'For God's sake,' Kieron swore angrily, 'I'm not going to tear him out of your arms and make off with him! What sort of man do you think I am?'

Her eyes gave him the answer. Just because Nicky was so precious to her it didn't necessarily mean that Kieron would feel the same way, and yet there had been something in his eyes when he looked at Nicky which made her heart pound with fear.

The moment Nicky saw the car he was wide-eyed with awe. Kieron insisted on holding him while Briony got in the back, handing him to her when she was sitting down.

'Okay, son?' he asked as he closed the door. The words were commonplace enough, but the look in his eyes made Briony go ice-cold with dread.

She was too concerned with Nicky's comfort to pay much attention to their surroundings, but when the car came to a stop outside an imposing block of apartments in the heart of Knightsbridge she glanced angrily at the back of Kieron's head. In the driving mirror his eyes met hers.

'We've got things to talk about,' he said softly.

Briony shivered. For a moment he had looked angry enough to kill her. 'I want to go home.'

He leaned behind her and opened the door. 'Out!'

They were in the lift before he spoke to her again, his eyes meeting hers over Nicky's curly head. The little boy had asked curiously where they were going, but had seemed quite satisfied with her answer that they were going to see Mr Blake's flat.

'I'll say one thing for you,' Kieron said curtly. 'At least you care about the child.'

'More than you could possibly know,' Briony breathed, not caring what she was betraying and missing entirely the thoughtful look in his eyes as he punched the buttons and the lift soared upwards.

His apartment was large and surprisingly comfortable. Kieron told her to make herself at home in the huge living room and disappeared into what she guessed to be the kitchen, emerging several minutes later with a glass of orange juice and a tray of coffee.

Nicky accepted the drink shyly. He had been unusually quiet in the car and Briony had put it down to his accident. Now, though, as she watched him staring solemnly at Kieron, it struck her that he must be shy. He was sitting on her lap and Kieron squatted down beside them, his eyes on a level with his son's.

'Are you a daddy?' Nicky asked him gravely.

Briony's muscles stiffened defensively, and she could not bring herself to look at Kieron.

'Yes,' he said quietly.

Nicky's shoulders hunched.

'I haven't got a daddy,' he said sorrowfully. 'But I want one, don't I, Mummy?'

Briony felt as though she wanted to die, or to have the ground open up and swallow her—preferably the former. A muscle twitched in Kieron's jaw and she couldn't tell whether he was angry or amused.

'Well, we'll have to see what we can do about that, son,' he said in a deep voice. 'Why don't you have a little sleep while your mummy and I talk about it?'

'Why did you have to say that to him?' Briony breathed angrily, when Nicky had been tucked up in Kieron's huge king-sized bed. To her surprise the little boy had evinced no concern at sleeping in the strange room, accepting Kieron's assurance that they would be within call.

'It's already hard enough for us. He's far too young to understand why he doesn't have a father. . . .'

'And young enough to forget that he ever did not,' Kieron replied in a clipped voice.

She fell back, clutching the deep leather settee.

'What do you mean?' But she already knew what he meant, and her eyes told him so.

'Nicky is my child, Briony, you can't deny it.'

'You fathered him, don't you mean?' Briony lashed back. 'But you have no other right to him.'

'No? I wonder what a court of law would say about that? He needs a father,' he said abruptly. 'Surely even you can see that?'

Her eyes dilated in fear, her voice choked.

'You're not going to take him away from me!'

He was watching her through narrowed eyes. 'It needn't come to that.'

What was he going to ask for? Visiting rights? She would never allow Nicky to be torn between them, and she would tell him so.

'We could always marry and provide our son with both his parents.'

Shock silenced her.

'Marry you?' she croaked when she had got her voice back. 'After what you did to me last time. Never!'

'I gave you Nicky,' he reminded her softly.

She moved away from him, sitting down on the settee and moving her head restlessly from side to side.

'Nicky and I don't need you.'

'You may not, but Nicky does,' he corrected. 'He needs a father.'

'Then I'll find him one,' Briony announced tartly, gasping in protest as his fingers fastened cruelly round her fingers. She had made a tactical error, and Kieron's eyes betrayed it. He would never let her give his son a stepfather.

'You little bitch!' he breathed angrily. 'You would do as well, just to spite me, wouldn't you? Well, two can play at that game. Nicky is my son and I want him badly enough to take you as well if I have to, but if you won't agree then I'll find Nicky another mother. One who can be at home with him all day to make sure he doesn't go falling out of trees,' he taunted cruelly. 'In custody cases the court's prime concern is for the child. I could give him the security of two parents; not a mother who has to leave him with child-minders while she goes out to work. I'm sure you don't need to use much imagination to know who the court would favour?'

How could he be so cruel? A sob rose in her throat, to be instantly suppressed. She must stay calm if she was to win the fight for Nicky. She must use logic and clear-sighted arguments.

'Until today you didn't even know he existed,' she persisted. 'How can you say you want him?'

'Didn't you, the first moment you set eyes on him?' he asked softly.

Her expression betrayed her.

'I'd never have given birth to him if I'd known it would come to this!' she spat bitterly, shocked into silence as he pulled her out of her seat and shook her until her teeth rattled.

'Don't ever let me hear you say that again!' he grated furiously. 'If I thought for a moment you meant it you'd be out of here before you could turn round—without my child!'

The unfairness of it all galled her. He had fathered Nicky without even knowing it, and yet here he was daring to accuse her of being an unfit mother.

'Marry me, Briony,' he said in a hard voice, 'otherwise I'll find someone else who will.'

'Give me time,' she said tiredly. 'I must do what's right for Nicky. Two quarrelling parents aren't. Surely you can see that, Kieron? Surely you can see that marriage between us might not necessarily be the best thing for Nicky?'

A sound from the bedroom drew her anxious eyes, but Kieron was there first, and when she went into the room he was sitting on the bed with Nicky. The little boy looked solemn and uncertain. His voice wobbled a little as he spoke her name, cuddling up against her as she took him in her arms. He pressed his face into her breasts, ignoring Kieron, and for a moment she felt triumph that he had turned from his father to her.

'I meant every word I said, Briony,' Kieron warned her quietly as she stood up with Nicky in her arms. 'I want your answer tomorrow. You can take the day off, that way you won't be able to accuse me of not giving you enough time to think.'

She was too engrossed in her own thoughts on the drive home to pay much attention to Nicky and was taken by surprise when, when the car stopped and Kieron came round to open the door, he demanded imperiously, 'Man carry me.' It infuriated her that Kieron did not even exhibit any triumph but merely lifted the little boy into his arms with a smile, Nicky's face split by an enormous grin as he laughed down at his father.

'Don't even begin to think about running out on me, Briony,' Kieron warned her as he put Nicky on his bed.

He followed her out into the living room, watching her unrelentingly as she stared out into the garden.

'This afternoon you were quite ready to think Nicky was Matt's,' she reminded him bitterly.

'And now I know he's mine I want to give you both the protection of my name.'

'Big of you,' Briony said savagely. 'But we don't need you, Kieron. And when we did, you weren't there.'

He went white at that. 'I didn't know you were pregnant, damn you! I've already tried to tell you. . . .'

'And I don't want to hear,' she interrupted, swinging round, her eyes burning with fury. 'Why are you doing this to us? Nicky and I were quite happy on our own.'

'You might have been, but was Nicky? A child needs two parents, Briony, and if you're honest you'll admit that. I only want what's best for him, just as you do. The moment I saw him and I knew that he was mine I realised I couldn't let him go out of my life. He is flesh of my flesh . . . bone of my bone. . . .'

'Conceived so that you could search the flat and find the evidence you needed to convict Myers,' she concluded bitterly. 'Oh get, out of here, you . . . you hypocrite!'

For a long time after he had gone she sat staring ahead of her, unaware that it had grown dark, or that Nicky's chatter had stilled, trying to come to terms with this fresh blow fate had struck her. Kieron had not been making idle threats. He would fight to get his child. And surely no court would favour the claims of a working mother over those of a father who could provide both a luxurious home and a suitable stepmother? Who did he have in mind? Gail? Hardly, the blonde girl disliked children intensely, but Kieron would never be short of women to share his life.

The faint rap on the door startled her and at first she thought it was Kieron. When she opened the door, though, it was Gina who stood there, her eyes red from crying.

'Oh, Gina, it wasn't your fault!' Briony exclaimed, hating herself for not going upstairs immediately upon her return. Had Gina thought she blamed her for the accident? 'I would have been up to see you, but I had things on my mind. Kieron wants us to be married, for Nicky's sake,' she said abruptly, not knowing why she felt this need to confide in someone.

Relief spread over Gina's face.

'Oh, Briony! Some good news at last! When we got back here from the hospital Paolo's papa was on the telephone. Paolo's elder brother has been seriously injured in a car accident and Papa Guido wants us to go home right away. With Cesare in hospital there will be no one to run the vineyard, and I was dreading telling you that we must leave.'

As she listened to her friend's story, Briony's heart sank. Of course Gina and Paolo would have to go home, but who would look after Nicky? How could she go out to work if she had no one she could trust to leave him with? He was far too young for nursery school; even if such facilities had existed locally. The only other alternative—which she shrank from—was finding a baby-minder who had room to take him, but she had always wanted Nicky to grow up in familiar surroundings, which was why she had been so glad to let Gina and Paolo have the flat. She could advertise for another couple, but that would take time, and even if she found someone suitable Nicky might not settle down with them as well as he had done with Gina, whom he had known since birth.

'Marriage!' Gina was saying romantically. 'Oh, that is so good! I knew the moment I saw him that he was not the man to turn his back on his own child. You quarrelled, *si*? and pride would not let you tell him about the baby. Oh, Paolo will be so relieved! We were dreading having to tell you. . . .'

Briony knew exactly what she meant. Somehow she could not find the words to tell Gina that she did not want to marry Kieron. She was trapped. And it seemed doubly ironic that it should be through the love she bore his child, whom he had not even known existed until today, and whom he had made it clear he intended to have beneath his roof and bearing his name, even if he had to destroy Nicky's mother to do so.

CHAPTER FIVE

'So the answer is yes?'

Kieron was standing with his back to her, staring out into the garden, his hands in the pockets on the hip-hugging dark trousers he was wearing. He had arrived just as she was putting Nicky to bed and the small sitting room was cluttered with the little boy's toys. His broken arm had kept him inside, and Briony had just been going to shower and change when Kieron's car slid to a halt outside.

She had been awake nearly all night, and close on twenty-four hours of arguing backwards and forwards with herself had left its effect. Her eyes looked huge in her small face, and she pushed the heavy mass of her copper hair back from her shoulders with a defeated gesture, unaware that Kieron had seen her reflection in the glass. He turned round, his eyes a deep, unfathomable navy blue, and Briony had to suppress the urge to snatch up Nicky and run as far and as fast as she could.

It was for Nicky's sake that she had been compelled to decide in favour of Kieron's proposal. It wasn't merely that he was better equipped than she to give Nicky material things; it was the fact that if she refused she would be deliberately depriving her child of his father—something for which Nicky might find it hard to forgive her later. Since his birth his well-being had been her prime concern, and little though she wanted the marriage it was impossible to deny its benefits for Nicky, even if it only meant that she would be able to spend more time with him.

If Gina and Paolo had not been leaving she might have found the courage to defy Kieron, but without them she knew she could not provide Nicky with the stable, loving background he needed. Constantly haunting her was the fear that Kieron would make good his threat to remove Nicky from her by legal means, and it showed in her haunted, shadowed eyes.

'I'm only agreeing for Nicky's sake,' she told Kieron bitterly.

'Of course.' The sardonic inflection troubled her. He seemed to dominate the small room, his motionless, watching stance sending shivers of fear trembling over her. She had been dreading his arrival all day, knowing that once she had committed herself there would be no escape. A heavy lethargy seemed to be pressing down on her.

'How soon. . . .' she began to ask, but although her lips formed the words, no sound could get past her tightly closed throat. She tried to speak again, panic clawing at her as Kieron swung round. His eyes narrowed, and she shrank back in fear as he walked over to where she was sitting. His face seemed to be dissolving above her. She heard words, but they had no meaning, reaching her through a wall of rushing water which grew louder and louder, and she felt herself falling into a bottomless black well.

'She's been overtaxing herself for years,' Briony heard a masculine voice proclaim above her with professional certainty. 'Looking after a lively two-year-old isn't a picnic at the best of times, and by the looks of it, she's been driving herself too hard.

Still, from what you tell me, things should be a little easier for her from now on.'

'Yes, we're getting married as soon as it can be arranged.'

'Umm. Well, I can't see any reason to delay that. Probably just the opposite. The sooner all the excitement's over and she can start to relax, the better.'

Briony moved restlessly, not liking being discussed as though she were an inanimate object. Kieron was standing beside her bed and registered the small movement, touching the doctor's arm.

'Well, young lady,' he exclaimed jovially, 'how do you feel now?'

'Weak,' Briony admitted. She was in her own bed, bright sunshine pouring in through the window, highlighting the overnight growth of stubble along Kieron's jaw.

'Nicky!' She struggled to sit up.

'Nicky's fine,' Kieron assured her curtly. 'I phoned an agency who specialise in emergencies like this. Mrs Johnson has taken Nicky out for a walk.'

The doctor was closing his case.

'What happened?' Briony asked him uncertainly. She felt curiously lightheaded, her body weightless almost.

'At a guess I'd say too many shocks on top of overwork and nervous strain. Your little boy had an accident, didn't he, and the shock you suffered then was probably the final straw for your nervous system. You wouldn't let it have the rest it needed, so it took matters into its own hands, and you blacked out. It isn't entirely uncommon, but it isn't to be recommended either, so from now on take things more

easily. Don't bottle everything up inside; the pressure
has to get out somehow, you know.'

He picked up his bag, and Kieron went with him
when he left the room.

Several hours of her life had vanished without
trace, Briony thought, shivering. She could remember a horrible sense of consciousness slipping
away and then nothing.

Her bedroom door opened and Kieron walked in.

'Do you feel well enough to talk?'

She nodded, her mouth dry. It had occurred to
her that her blackout might have been an attempt
to escape from Kieron and their marriage, and she
glanced uncertainly at him. She was wearing a short
cotton nightdress, and had no memory of putting it
on herself.

'Did you . . . did you undress me?'

He eyed her with wry comprehension. 'Don't
panic. I didn't attempt to slake my animalistic
desires on your defenceless body, if that's what's
worrying you.' His eyes slid over her prone form,
glinting faintly as they returned to her flushed face.
'I've made all the arrangements for the wedding,' he
told her calmly. 'Mrs Johnson will look after Nicky
for the day. I've arranged for her to pack his clothes
and yours. I don't want a repeat performance of last
night—it wouldn't exactly look good if my bride
fainted away at my feet.' He ran a hand along his
jaw. 'I don't suppose you have such a thing as a
razor, do you? I went upstairs to see if I could borrow
one from Paolo, but I couldn't get any answer.'

'They've had to go back to Italy. Paolo's brother
is seriously ill.'

'We'll need to look for a house,' Kieron com-

mented coolly, 'but that will have to wait until
you're feeling better. You and Nicky can move into
my apartment for the time being. I don't intend to
spend any more nights on your settee. I like to
sleep—and make love—in slightly more comfortable
surroundings these days.'

Briony's lips compressed into a bitter line. 'There
won't be any "making love" between us, Kieron,
and moving into your apartment is out of the question. Nicky needs a garden to play in. You can't
coop up a boisterous child in a flat.'

'No "making love"? Shouldn't you wait until
you're asked?' Kieron drawled softly. 'If the apartment's out, what did you have in mind? There isn't
room for the three of us here.' He glanced disparagingly round her small bedroom, his glance en-
compassing the narrow single bed. 'Or were you
hoping to relegate me to the other flat?'

It was exactly what Briony had had in mind. Her
hands shook as she gripped them together beneath
the bedclothes. His earlier sardonic comment about
her 'waiting to be asked' had touched a raw nerve,
and she was in no condition to argue with him.

'Your using the upstairs flat would be a sensible
solution,' she pointed out, trying to appear logical.
'Nicky isn't properly used to you yet. . . .'

'No! We're getting married to provide Nicky with
a proper family, not a father who lives in a separate
flat with visiting rights doled out sparingly by you.
If you don't want to live in the flat then we'll find a
house.'

'Then couldn't we put off the wedding until we
do?'

Her mouth had gone dry, her eyes sliding away

from Kieron's as she prayed that he would agree, but he did not.

'No way,' he told her softly. 'In three days' time we're getting married, even if I have to carry you to the altar. It's all arranged. I've even got the licence.' He pushed back the cuff of his jacket. 'I've got to go to the office. Mrs Johnson will be back soon and she's got strict instructions not to let you set a foot out of bed.'

Mrs Johnson proved to be a motherly, very capable woman in her late thirties who carried out Kieron's instructions to the letter. Nicky was allowed into his mother's room at lunch-time to share her lunch tray as a special treat, and he chattered blithely to Briony while she picked at her chicken salad.

'I'm going to have a daddy soon,' he told her importantly, 'and we're going to go and live with him in a new house.'

Kieron hadn't wasted much time in informing his son of the changes to come, Briony reflected bitterly. Couldn't he have left that to her? Or didn't he trust her to do it without prejudicing Nicky against him? Resentment washed over her. She wanted only what was best for her child, and she could never do anything which might affect him adversely.

Nicky had been so used to having her all to himself, she wasn't sure how he would react to a third member of their small family. It wasn't unknown for small boys to resent a male intruder into their mother's life, but of course their circumstances were not such that Nicky would have to witness any unaccustomed intimacy between herself and Kieron. For the first time she was curious about Kieron's feelings about their marriage. Marriage to her precluded him from having the things a man normally looked for in marriage. Did he think Nicky would compensate for what he was missing, or was it that he was cynically thinking that in view of their shared animosity he could continue to live the life of a bachelor where women were concerned? She was shocked by the intensity of her anger. What did it matter to her what Kieron did with his life?

At teatime she felt well enough to get up, but Mrs Johnson was adamant that she should not. She had made Nicky bread and butter soldiers to eat with his egg, and Nicky was dipping these enthusiastically into the yoke when Briony pushed open the kitchen door.

'Mr Blake told me that you were not to get up on any account,' she protested.

'Mr Blake doesn't give the orders round here,' Briony replied tartly. Her hair felt untidy and tacky and she wanted to wash it. Besides, lying in bed gave her too much time to think.

When Nicky had finished his tea, she thanked Mrs Johnson for her help and firmly dismissed her. Nicky chattered happily while she bathed him, and they played all his favourite games. It was amazing how much more he seemed to learn every day, Briony thought fondly, listening to him telling her all about his day.

'When will my daddy be coming?' he demanded suddenly.

Kieron had not said when he would return. He had told her next to nothing about the arrangements for the wedding. If he did not ring her tomorrow she would have to phone him, Briony decided unwillingly. Nicky was staring up at her uncertainly and she took a deep breath, telling herself that she must start preparing her son for the changes to come.

'I don't know when exactly,' she began carefully. 'Soon, probably.'

'And then we'll be going to live with him for ever?'

'I expect so.' She lifted him out of the bath, briskly towelling his squirming, solid little body, and tickling him playfully.

'Won't we be living here any more?' he asked her suddenly, his forehead puckering. 'Will we be going away like Gina?'

'Perhaps. Now come on. Which story shall we read tonight?' she asked him.

She tucked him up in bed with one of his books while she went to wash her own hair and shower, towelling her thick curls briskly before pulling on a thin robe and padding back to his bedroom.

She had just reached the end of the story when the bedroom door opened and Kieron walked in, pulling off his jacket which he flung across the bed, loosening his tie, the oddly intimate gesture tightening her throat with tension.

Kieron smiled briefly at Nicky, who was watching him round-eyed and uncertain. Briony closed the book, not surprised to see that her hands were shaking. There was something she had to do now which would cause her the most bitter agony, but for Nicky's sake she must. Bending over the bed, she said softly to her son:

'Look who's here, Nicky—it's your daddy.'

There was a tension-filled moment when she felt Kieron's incredulous stare and Nicky's uncertain one, and then Kieron was sitting next to her on the bed, his eyes on his son's face as he said huskily, 'Hello, Nicky.'

When she closed the bedroom door behind her, there were tears in Briony's eyes. She couldn't remember a time when anything had caused her quite so much pain, unless it was the discovery of Kieron's deceit, and she had to bite her lip to prevent herself from crying out loud. What was Kieron saying to Nicky? Was he trying to poison the little boy's mind against her?

She went into her own bedroom, plugging in her hair-dryer and brushing her hair, the activity helping to disperse her restless thoughts.

They could not be held back for ever, though, and she was on her knees, her head in her hands, the hairdryer whirring away unregarded at her side, when Kieron walked in.

He was beside her before she was aware of his presence, her eyes moving slowly along his lean length, as he gripped her arms to pull her upwards.

'Thanks,' he said softly. 'That was a very generous thing you did.'

'Nicky?'

If he heard her anxiety and guessed the reason for it, he gave no sign.

'He's asleep.' His fingers touched her cheek, and when he turned them over they were damp with her tears.

'Oh, Briony,' he protested softly, gathering her up against him, 'is marriage to me so abhorrent to you that it makes you cry?'

'I'm not,' she retorted, but the words were lost against his chest. She hadn't cried in years and she hated herself for the weakness that made her do so now, but now she had started it didn't seem possible to stop. She wanted to tell Kieron to let her go, but her body seemed to mould itself treacherously to his as though drawing strength from his masculine frame while Kieron's soft reassurances were murmured into her hair. As though her tears were the melting ice which had frozen her heart, she could feel her body coming to life beneath his stroking hands, sensations she had completely forgotten surging up inside her. Kieron's hands found their way inside her robe, caressing her quivering flesh, emotions dammed up for years clamouring urgently for satisfaction as she yielded mindlessly to his touch, her will-power over-ridden by a primeval need that nothing could stem.

She reached blindly towards him, tracing the heard bones of his shoulders, barely aware of him shrugging impatiently out of his shirt and lifting her to carry her to the narrow bed.

Her mouth parted on a soft groan, her whole body shuddering deeply in response to his kiss, her body moving passionately against him, until he cupped her hands and held her away from him, his voice husky and unsteady.

'No one's touched you in years, have they?' he demanded incredulously. 'It's all been waiting there, dammed up behind the ice, just needing a touch to set it free. Well, it's free now,' he groaned against her skin, pulling her against his hard body, 'Feel what you're doing to me, Briony. I want to make love to you, but this time without deceit. I'm not going to be accused of that twice.'

His words shattered through the partition she had

erected between her mind and body, forcing her mind to accept the actions of her flesh, and she cringed back from him immediately, her face white and sick.

'What the hell?' Kieron stared down at her. 'Don't tease me, Briony,' he commanded. 'I don't like it, and you may find out you've bitten off more than you can chew. For a moment there you were a woman. You can't wall her up for ever. Some time or other she's going to break through and play havoc with your emotionless little world.'

Horror engulfed her. What had happened to her? She had reacted to Kieron's touch like brushwood to tinder. She pushed him away, sick with self-revulsion. Oh, God, what must he be thinking? She couldn't possibly marry him now. White with self-loathing, she stared up at him, her eyes blazing defiantly.

'Well, go on, then,' she hurled at him. 'Gloat! That's what you're doing inside, isn't it? Thinking how easy it was to turn me on? Oh, God, how I hate you!'

Kieron's face was nearly as white as her own.

'Is that what you think?' he demanded furiously. 'That I'd deliberately and coldbloodedly do something like that?'

How long they stared at one another in mutual bitterness, Briony did not know. She only knew that when she eventually managed to drag her eyes away from him she was shaking uncontrollably.

'You did it once before,' she reminded him bitterly.

'And since then you haven't allowed a man into your life, is that it?'

She laughed then, sobering only when he shook her hard. 'What's so funny?' he demanded harshly.

'I've let one man into my life,' she reminded him. 'Your son. The reason we have to go through this farce of a marriage.'

'It's too late to back out now,' he warned her. 'Nicky. . . .'

'Yes, I know. It's for Nicky's sake that I'm doing this. I want that understood plainly, Kieron. I won't be degraded by lovemaking without love again.'

He studied her for a few minutes, his expression unreadable, and then the colour drained from her face as he said slowly.

'And if it was with love?'

Her mind rejected the words instantly, only the terrible aching of her body confirming that she wasn't entirely free of the past. She clamped down on the feeling.

'I don't love you!'

The ring of the telephone broke the tension-filled silence like a gunshot. Kieron got off the bed and went into the living room, leaving Briony to fasten her robe and pad resentfully after him.

'It was for me,' he told her calmly, replacing the receiver. 'I gave the paper your number.'

Who had it been? Gail? Why should she care?

'Something's cropped up and I've got to get down there,' Kieron told her as though he had sensed her suspicions. 'What I came to tell you is that I think I've managed to find us a house. Some friends of mine who live in Surrey are going to the States for twelve months and they're prepared to let their house to us, which should give us time to look round for what we really want. It will also mean that you

aren't exhausting yourself going round estate agents'
offices. What are you going to do about clothes?'

The question caught her off guard.

'What do you mean?' she asked stiffly.

His impatient sigh rustled through the space between them.

'I mean do you want me to organise someone to
look after Nicky while you go out and buy yourself a
wedding dress? Look, I'm not suggesting white with
all the trimmings,' he said hardily when she flinched,
'but most women seem to consider marriage an
excuse for buying themselves a new outfit.'

'Well, I'm not most women,' Briony said tartly.
'If I wore something appropriate to my mood, I'd
probably be dressed in sackcloth and ashes!'

For a moment she thought she had gone too far.
Something blazed angrily in his eyes, but as she took
a step backwards it faded, to be replaced by a faintly
mocking smile, which strangely enough annoyed her
more than his anger.

'You really do believe in making things hard for
yourself, don't you?' he said softly. 'Tomorrow you
will go out and buy yourself something to be married
in. And if you don't, I shall personally make sure
that you do, even if it means stripping you myself
and putting your clothes on you. Do you understand?'

He was gone before she could retaliate, leaving
her exhausted and drained and yet, curiously, more
alive than she had felt in years.

Kieron certainly didn't believe in doing things by
halves, Briony thought lightheadedly as she sipped
her champagne. She had had no idea until after the

ceremony that Kieron had arranged a reception at
the Savoy.

The wedding itself had been a surprise too. She
had somehow expected a simple register office service, and had been caught off guard when the taxi
Kieron had organised for her stopped outside her
local church.

There had been a moment when they had been
making their vows when she had thought fleetingly
of how different it could all have been if Kieron
had been the man she had once thought, but she
had banished it as being stupidly romantic, concen-
trating instead of the real reasons for their alliance.

'Well, well, you are a dark horse, aren't you?'
Gail eyed her assessingly. 'Who would have thought
it?'

'Who would have thought what?' Kieron drawled,
suddenly materialising at Briony's side, the arm he
slid deliberately round her waist making her stiffen,
her eyes flashing resentfully.

'Cross already, sweetheart?' His mouth laughed,
but his eyes were warning her against defiance. 'I
promise I'll stay right here at your side for the rest
of the day—and the night.'

Anger burned up under her skin, Gail forgotten as
she turned impulsively towards him intending to
demand that he let her go, but her objections were
stifled under the warmth of his mouth, his voice a
silky whisper as he murmured:

'Remember, we've just been married. Everyone
expects us to look happy. It's all very romantic. You
don't want everyone thinking I was forced to marry
you to give Nicky a name, do you? Because that's
what they'll think.'

It was on the tip of her tongue to tell him that she didn't care, but she swallowed the impetuous words.

'Goodness, Kieron, I never realised you were so demonstrative,' Gail said with a brittle smile. 'And I thought I knew you so well!' She flashed Briony a look of pure malice and added softly, 'Is it true, Briony, that you have a child? I couldn't believe it when Kieron told me. I've always thought of you as such a little goody-goody. Heaven knows what poor Matt will do when he hears! He's practically distraught with the news that you and Kieron are marrying.'

'Not "a child", Gail,' Kieron's deep voice drawled, 'but my child.' Briony felt him look at her. 'I suppose we'd better make a clean breast of it, darling, we can't hide something like Nicky.'

Briony's hands clenched into small fists. The falsity of the situation sickened her. When she had agreed to marry him she had never dreamed that she would be expected to play the part of the blushing bride.

'Don't stop there,' Gail urged. 'Heavens, it all sounds like a fairy story!'

'Not really,' Kieron shrugged. 'Briony and I quarrelled before she knew she was expecting Nicky, and she was too proud to tell me what had happened. When I came back to this country and we met again, we found ourselves falling in love with one another for a second time, and the discovery that Briony had had my child was the final gilt to the gingerbread.'

'Kieron tells me you're giving up work,' Gail said to Briony, who had remained silent through Kieron's highly edited version of what had happened. 'Won't you be bored to tears?'

Briony stiffened, resenting her patronising tone, but Kieron answered for her, his eyes gleaming with amusement as he looked down at her flushed face.

'Oh, I think we could find a remedy for that,' he said smoothly. 'We don't want Nicky to be an only child.'

Briony was glad that someone else claimed Gail's attention. 'I don't. . . .' she began heatedly, only to be silenced by the firm fingers Kieron laid against her lips.

'No man likes being laughed at,' he told her. 'I want it clearly understood that Nicky is my child, just as I want it clearly understood that you are now my wife. I like the outfit, by the way,' he added carelessly, his eyes resting deliberately on the soft swell of her breasts beneath her cream silk suit.

She had told herself that she would not buy anything special, but somehow or other she had found herself buying this silk chiffon three-piece with its pencil-slim skirt and brief camisole top under a delicately pleated long-sleeved jacket. The pale colour set off her hair, making it seem more red than usual and her eyes a more vivid green, and as Kieron looked at her she was uncomfortably conscious that beneath the thin chiffon top she was wearing nothing at all. The camisole was too brief and thin to wear over a bra, and in impatient haste when she dressed she had worn it without giving a thought to any possible consequences.

'Mm, it's very nice,' Kieron drawled softly as though he had read her thoughts.

'You shouldn't have told Gail about Nicky,' Briony protested, trying to change the subject.

His eyes glinted with anger.

'Why not? Nicky might be a dark secret to you, but not to me. I'm proud of my son and I don't care who knows that I fathered him.'

His chauvinism infuriated her.

'I don't suppose you care about them knowing how you fathered him either, do you? You're practically inhuman! You expect me to behave as though this were the happiest day of my life, when all the time you've forced me into this marriage to prevent you from taking my son—a son that you fathered without thought or love, or any other emotion except ambition. Your arrogance is astounding! I. . . .'

Her words were smothered by his mouth, the hard, angry pressure of his hands bruising her skin through the thin chiffon. She could hear people laughing and cheering, and when Kieron released her she was chagrined to discover that they were the centre of a small crowd of grinning onlookers.

Someone claimed Kieron's attention, and he turned aside to talk to them. Most of their guests were people from the paper. There were one or two people Kieron had introduced as old friends, and Briony had endured their curious inspection with as much fortitude as she could muster.

Mrs Johnson was looking after Nicky, and already she was fretting to get back to him. Ever since his accident she worried whenever she was away from him, and Kieron had already rebuked her once for fussing over him.

She had been bitterly angry, resenting his assumption that he had an equal right to say what was best for Nicky, and now her stomach lurched protestingly as she realised that marriage to him had given him that right.

She wandered away, deep in thought, not realising until he caught her arm that Matt had been following her. He looked thin and unhappy, and she was consumed with guilt at not letting him know what was happening.

'I couldn't believe it,' he reproached her. 'Briony, what am I going to do without you? No one listens to me but you.'

She almost laughed out loud at his childish self-absorption, realising with new clarity that his appeal had been similar to Nicky's, only far weaker, and that it had been his dependence upon her which had relaxed her barriers, as though she had known instinctively that he would never represent the same threat to her defences that Kieron did.

'I miss you so much, Briony,' he mumbled. 'I wanted to talk to you. I don't know what to do. Should I take Mary back?'

If he had to ask her he couldn't be very sure of his feelings, Briony thought in exasperation. She was just about to tell him that he would have to make his own decisions, when a dark shadow loomed, and she glanced up to find Kieron bearing down on them, his face grim and unsmiling.

'Briony is my wife now,' he told Matt angrily, grasping her wrist painfully tightly. 'Just remember that. And as for you,' he grated to Briony as Matt shrank back, 'what the hell do you think you're playing at? I haven't gone to all this trouble to convince everyone that we're a pair of deliriously happy reunited lovers just to have you sabotage everything by letting that idiot weep all over you!'

The intensity of his anger shocked her into silence.

'Matt and I are old friends,' she protested when she had found her voice. 'No one would ever think that. . . .'

'You were lovers?' Kieron grated. 'You'd be surprised. I thought you were myself, until I found out you were virtually untouched. . . .'

'Like the Sleeping Beauty awaiting the Prince's kiss?' Briony flung at him. 'Is that what you think, Kieron? That you only have to touch me and I'll waken up? I'm sorry to have to disappoint you. I'm frozen all the way through.'

'You melted the other night,' he reminded her softly, watching her eyes so that there was no way she could conceal her shock wave of reaction.

'I didn't know what I was doing,' she countered bravely. 'Nicky's accident . . . the shock. . . .'

'Yes, I know all about that,' he agreed harshly. 'You don't need to put into words that you wouldn't have let me within fifty miles of you if your defences hadn't been cracked wide open. But they aren't unbreachable. Remember that next time you feel like defying me!'

He turned on his heel before she could respond, leaving her feeling stricken by the realisation that he had spoken the truth. Where Kieron was concerned she was dangerously vulnerable, and she would have to work ceaselessly to ensure that her defences were never breached again. She had already endured the galling bitterness of lovemaking without love once; she could not survive that agony again.

CHAPTER SIX

THEY left the reception in a shower of rice and confetti, to the tune of goodnatured teasing from their colleagues, although Briony noticed that neither Gail nor Matt was there to wave them off.

'I didn't think you'd thank me for organising a honeymoon,' Kieron said sardonically as they drove out of London. 'Although seeing you dressed—or should I say undressed—like that is giving me second thoughts.'

'Then forget them,' Briony said crisply. 'You told me to buy a new outfit and I did.'

'What a pity you can't always be so delightfully obedient,' Kieron mocked. 'Where am I to sleep tonight, by the way, or can I guess?'

A deep flush mantled Briony's cheeks. They had decided to move down to the house Kieron was renting from his friends the day after the wedding took place, and to Briony's surprise Kieron had raised no objections to her insistence that she and Nicky stayed in her own house until then. However, her poppy-flushed cheeks were the result of a last-minute quixotic impulse this morning before the taxi arrived with Mrs Johnson which had taken her upstairs to the upper flat's double bedroom, which was still furnished, where she had made the bed up with fresh sheets and placed a clean nightdress conspicuously across it. The moment Mrs Johnson arrived she regretted the foolish gesture. What on earth did it

matter what the woman thought of her marriage?—
but with her own taxi at the door it had been too
late to run upstairs and rectify her mistake.

'Perhaps Nicky will let you share his bed?' she
suggested with a touch of humour.

'Or perhaps his mummy will let me share hers?'

'No!'

'So vehement,' Kieron mocked gently. 'I seem to
remember a time when you couldn't wait for me to
share your bed.'

Briony was too chagrined to look at him. How
could she survive their marriage if he was constantly
going to be throwing the past in her face?

'Perhaps what you taught me there made me want
to ensure that there was never a repeat performance!'
she threw at him to conceal her embarrassment.

The car suddenly screeched to a halt, flinging her
hard against the passenger door, the blow knocking
the breath from her body. Kieron's hands were on
her shoulders, his eyes glittering with fury as he
pulled her towards him.

'Don't you ever accuse me of anything like that
again!' he muttered menacingly through gritted
teeth. 'Or I really will give you something to com-
plain about. And while we're here. . . .'

His mouth covered hers bruisingly, his hands in
her hair, tangling the curls. The kiss robbed her of
breath, hard and angry in its demand, and then he
released her and thrust her back into her seat.

'Now you look as though you've just got married,'
he grated with satisfaction.

'I'm sure Mrs Johnson will be most impressed,'
Briony said bitterly. 'But you needn't have bothered.
Other people's impressions don't worry me.'

Briony had done her best to prepare Nicky for their new life. He had been told about the wedding, but had expressed little interest, being far more concerned with when his daddy was actually coming to live with them.

Already he doted on Kieron, and Briony had suffered several pangs of jealousy watching them together. Already, in a few brief days, Nicky seemed to have grown from a baby to a little boy.

He toddled out of the house the moment the car stopped, suffering Briony's swift hug with impatience before turning to his father and demanding to be carried.

'I'll put him to bed,' she said over her shoulder to Kieron as they entered the house. 'Why don't you give Mrs Johnson a lift home?'

'On your wedding night?' the latter exclaimed. 'I wouldn't dream of it!'

'How about letting me put Nicky to bed?' Kieron suggested when she had gone.

'Can't you be content with being his father?' Briony lashed out at him. 'Must you usurp my role as well?'

'You mistook my intention,' Kieron said quietly, his body suddenly tense. He had been putting Nicky on the floor, and as though sensing the anger in the adult voices the little boy whimpered protestingly and clung to Kieron's legs.

'You looked tired. The doctor said you weren't to overdo things. You hardly ate a thing at the reception. I was going to suggest that I put Nicky to bed while you rested, and that then I made us an omelette.'

'Oh, for God's sake, Kieron, stop the play-acting!'

All at once her self-control snapped. Was Kieron deliberately trying to make her feel guilty and unreasonable? If so he was succeeding. Even Nicky was looking at her with a frown in his dark blue eyes. 'I'll see to Nicky. . . .' she began, and then remembering the yet-to-be-attended-to upstairs bedroom, changed her mind and said flatly, 'Oh, what's the use? You do it if you must, only don't bother with an omelette for me. If I had to eat anything I'd choke!'

She let herself out of the flat while Kieron and Nicky were in the bathroom.

Upstairs the evening sun poured into the comfortable double bedroom, shining through the thin cotton nightdress she had placed on the bed. She was just reaching it when the door opened, and Kieron's exasperated voice said, 'So there you are! Nicky wants his duck and I. . . .'

She had her back to him, but she knew the instant he saw the nightdress, because his voice suddenly changed, sharp with disbelief, and it didn't need his soft, 'Well, well, it seems as though I am going to have a wedding night after all,' to warn her what a precarious position she had placed herself in.

'I put it there because of Mrs Johnson,' she began defensively,

'You did? A woman who not two hours ago was telling me that she didn't give a damn about other people's impressions? I don't believe you.'

'Believe what you damned well like. I wouldn't sleep with you willingly if you were the last man on earth!'

'You wouldn't get the chance,' Kieron replied brutally, 'if that shapeless cotton sack is the nearest you can get to wearing something enticing.' His fingers flicked disparagingly at the garment in question, high-necked and faded from numerous washings, and hurt tears stung Briony's eyes, although why she should be hurt she could not have said, but as though his contemptuous words had touched a deep buried nerve she quivered with mingled pain and indignation, longing to deliver an equally effective snub back. The nearest she could get to it was to demand breathlessly, 'I don't suppose you sleep in anything?'

'Certainly not,' he agreed suavely. 'And I haven't had any complaints as yet.'

As she stalked towards the door, he caught her by the arm, his eyes mocking and intent.

'Was it just for Mrs Johnson's sake, Briony?' he asked softly. 'Or was that woman you've tried to bury so deeply making her presence felt again?'

'I don't know what you mean!'

The way he was looking at her was making her feel oddly breathless, her skin quivering under the lazy circling caress of his thumb against its softness. She tried to avoid his eyes, staring instead straight in front of her, which was a mistake, for all she could see was the hard expanse of his chest and the dark hair curling crisply there, all sorts of treacherous memories suddenly surfacing with devastating clarity.

'I've got to go to Nicky,' she mumbled huskily. 'Please let go of me.'

He released her, but did not move away, and she was unbearably conscious of the maleness of him as she brushed past his motionless body, her face on fire with anger at the deliberately enforced intimacy.

'But *how* soon will we be there?' Nicky demanded for the third time. They were sitting in Kieron's car heading for the new house. Briony had not made her mind up what to do about her own and Kieron had suggested that for the time being they let the flats on a temporary basis, fully furnished, until she came to a decision.

She had hardly slept, and Nicky's excited chatter filled the silence which seemed to stretch between herself and Kieron. She had gone straight to bed as soon as Nicky was asleep, claiming that she was exhausted, despite Kieron's request that they talk. What did they have to talk about, she wondered bitterly, apart from their son?

It was still early enough in the summer for the countryside to be fresh and green, despite the long weeks without rain, and in any other circumstances Briony would have enjoyed the outing. The powerful car ate up the miles, the air-conditioning maintaining a pleasantly cool temperature, but although she tried to concentrate on the passing landscape Briony found it impossible to relax.

The house was in a small village, Kieron had told her, adding that he would do something about getting her a small car so that she could get about. As she knew from working with Doug a newspaper editor's life was subject to a good many pressures and demands, not the least of which was being called out at any time of the night or day when emergencies arose, and surely Kieron would prefer to be closer to the centre of town.

When she voiced these doubts he shrugged them aside, saying that the house was only a temporary measure, adding glintingly, 'Planning on how fast you can get rid of me, already?'

She didn't know how she was going to endure his constant presence; after one day the pressure of striving for normalcy was beginning to tell on her to such an extent that she felt continually on edge; tearful and nervy, ready even to snap at poor little Nicky.

Although they found the village without any problems, Kieron had to stop and ask the way to the house. It was down a narrow, rutted lane, a black and white timber building with a thatched roof and latticed windows peering out from beneath thatched eaves. A cat basked on the worn flags flanked by lavender bushes, and Briony caught her breath in disbelieving wonder, turning spontaneously to Kieron to comment shakily, 'It's beautiful!'

'It was an old Tudor barn before it was renovated, and extended,' Kieron informed her, stopping the car. 'The garden's a bit on the large side, although I'm given to understand that a gardener goes with the place. Apparently there's even a swing in the back garden for Nicky. That should keep you climbing out of any more apple trees,' he told his son.

They all got out of the car, Kieron producing some keys from his pocket and unfastening the gate, which Briony was relieved to see had a proper catch. Nicky was inclined to be over-adventurous at times, and she would have to watch that he didn't stray.

She and Nicky followed Kieron up the path, Nicky tugging free of her restraining hand to run up to the basking cat, exclaiming with pleasure, 'Pussy!'

The cat endured his attentions for several seconds with basilisk eyes before stretching and disappearing into the shrubbery, but by then a butterfly had caught Nicky's fascinated attention, and he was toddling hurriedly after that. Kieron had unlocked the front door, and Briony made to walk past him, gasping with indignation as he suddenly swung her up in his arms.

'What are you doing with my mummy?'

It was the first time Nicky had showed any signs of possessiveness, his dark blue eyes as stormily angry as his father's could be as he stood in front of them.

'I'm carrying her over the threshold of our very first home. Perhaps other aspects of our union haven't been quite as custom dictates,' Kieron drawled to Briony, 'but I see no reason why this one shouldn't be, do you?'

'Put me down!' Briony demanded.

'Why?' he mocked. 'Are you frightened that I might carry you up those stairs and demand those conjugal rights you promised me yesterday? With my body. . . .' he reminded her softly.

Nicky, impatient of these adult discussions, tugged impatiently at Kieron's trousers.

'Put my mummy down!' he demanded.

With a mocking look at Briony Kieron complied. 'Have you been teaching him to say that?' he taunted.

To her relief the cottage had three good-sized bedrooms. Kieron came upstairs while she was unpacking Nicky's things in the smallest of them.

'Is it too much to hope that you'll perform the same service for me?'

Briony pretended not to have heard him. It did odd things to her pulse rate to think of touching his clothes—clothes which had been worn next to his flesh.

The days fell into a similar pattern. Despite his faint stirrings of jealousy Nicky was devoted to his father, and Briony normally got up early with Kieron so that the little boy could see him before he left for work. Since their arrival at the cottage, Kieron had become far more distant and there were no more of those barbed comments she had come to dread. Often it was late when he got home, and then he started spending odd nights in the flat in London. Briony told herself that she was glad. She could sleep far more easily when he wasn't there, and yet that wasn't true. She found it ridiculously difficult to sleep when he was away, and Nicky got fractious, demanding to know when his daddy was coming back.

One evening the phone rang and a man asked for Kieron, introducing himself as the owner of the cottage. He sounded most anxious to know how they had settled in, and on impulse when he had rung off, Briony dialled the number of the London flat, intending to tell Kieron about the call.

The phone rang for a long time, and she was just about to hang up when someone picked up the receiver, and a female voice called, 'I've got it, darling, I expect it's the paper. What a time to ring!'

Briony recognised the voice instantly as Gail's and hung up quietly. She didn't know why the knowledge that Gail was with her husband in his flat should cause her such bitter pain that she wanted to scream with the agony of it, but it did.

'Mummy sad?' Nicky asked sorrowfully.

Kieron returned home the following night, and

although Briony had told herself that she would simply behave as though the phone call had never happened, she found it impossible even to speak to him.

He flung his jacket over a chair, wrenching off his tie and dropping into a chintz-covered chair, with a weary, 'God, I'm tired!'

'Perhaps you should try sleeping more often,' Briony said sweetly.

His eyes had been closed, and suddenly they flew open, nearly black with anger and exhaustion.

'And just what the hell is that supposed to mean?' he asked bitingly. 'A red-blooded man has certain needs and tensions and if they aren't satisfied he sometimes finds it damned hard to sleep—but of course you wouldn't know anything about that, would you?' he taunted.

They had supper in stony silence, Briony getting up the moment the meal was over to stack the dishes in the dishwasher and tidy up the kitchen. When she went back to the living room Kieron was fast asleep, his features oddly vulnerable and more like Nicky's than ever. Telling herself that it was merely that resemblance that tugged so insidiously at her heart, she hardened it against him and went upstairs. Let him sleep down there if he liked! She wasn't going to wake him.

She heard the phone ringing through a fog of sleep, dimly, without actually waking up, and in the morning there was a note propped up against a milk bottle telling her that Kieron had been called out by the paper.

'Thanks for the TLC,' he had scribbled sarcastically on the bottom of it, and she crumpled it up angrily, and flung it in a wastepaper basket.

What was the point of Kieron insisting on marrying her so that he could be a father to Nicky, when even at weekends he went to work, she thought savagely, refusing to acknowledge that it wasn't merely the little boy who suffered during his father's absence.

As much to work off her bad temper as anything else she dressed in old jeans and a tee-shirt, spending most of the morning weeding one of the large flower beds, while Nicky toddled about close by chattering happily to himself. He was an imaginative child, and listening to his mysterious monologue Briony felt a renewal of all her love for him.

By lunchtime her back and legs were aching from bending over, and after tidying up the weeds she took Nicky in for a rest, while she showered.

The sound of a car in the lane brought her rushing to the window, her hair still damp as she pulled on a thin silk robe, but it was Matt who was walking up the garden path, not Kieron.

She ran downstairs to let him in, too suprised by his unexpected arrival to question what he was doing there. If anything he looked more dejected than ever.

'It's Mary,' he told her unhappily when Briony had made him a cup of tea. 'She's threatening to leave me again. She complains that I'm boring and that I never take her anywhere. But how can I? Kieron works us like galley slaves. Our circulation has shot up these last few weeks, but he says he won't rest until he's made the *Globe* the best selling paper in the country. I'm so tired out when I get home that all I want to do is fall asleep, but Mary just can't seem to understand.'

He looked almost ready to burst into tears, and
Briony had to suppress a wave of irritation. No
wonder Mary was able to bully him so easily—his
apathetic lack of self-confidence was enough to drive
a saint mad.

'Look, you must explain to her how busy you are,'
Briony told him. 'Either that or find yourself a job
that will be less taxing.'

'You think like she does, don't you?' he accused
bitterly. 'You've changed, Briony. You used to
understand, but now you're just like all the others.
Perhaps I ought to act more like Kieron,' he said
wildly, grabbing hold of her before she could stop
him. 'Perhaps I ought to just take what I want.'

'Matt, let me go at once!' Briony demanded, more
cross than frightened. 'Don't be silly. I haven't
changed at all. I just think that now you and Mary
are back together you ought to try and make the
best of it.'

She sensed that the anger had gone out of him,
but instead of releasing her, he bowed his head on
her shoulder, his voice thick with tears. 'Oh God,
Briony, I'm sorry.'

'You will be, if you don't get out of here right
now,' Kieron said icily from the door. As Matt
stepped awkwardly back Kieron's eyes moved slowly
over Briony's thinly clad body, missing nothing, his
face rigid with an anger that made her stomach
churn in protesting fear.

Matt stumbled towards the door after one look at
Kieron's set face, his eyes sliding uncomfortably
away from Briony's as she willed him to explain what
had happened.

'And if you so much as set one foot here again, I'll

personally tear you limb from limb!' Kieron warned him harshly opening the door.

When Matt had gone, the silence in the kitchen seemed to stretch like taut wire, and only when they heard his car engine fire did Kieron look contemptuously at the empty tea-cups and drawl sardonically:

'I've heard of people enjoying a cigarette afterwards, but tea? Typical of Matt, though. Is that really what you like, or is it just that with Matt you feel safe because you're the boss?'

When Briony didn't speak he gritted at her, 'My God, what are you trying to do? Prove to me that I'm not the only man who can father a child on you? Well, if that's the case, I'd better make sure that we'll never know who *is* responsible for the second one!'

He reached for her before she could stop him, palms flat against the wall, trapping her against it, his eyes shredding her defences.

'Kieron, you don't understand. Matt. . . .' she protested, but he wasn't listening, his eyes curiously blind as he picked her up and moved determinedly towards the stairs, ruthlessly pinioning her wrists as she attempted to struggle free.

'I don't want to know,' he said thickly as they reached the landing. Her bedroom was closest and he kicked open the door, dropping her on the bed and pinning her there with the full weight of his body, one hand coolly parting her robe while the other held her flailing arms captive.

'Does *he* look at you like this?' he demanded huskily, his eyes drinking in the sight of her pale flesh. 'God, I'd almost forgotten!' The words died away as he bent and unerringly found the small mole beneath her breast. Her heart pounded frantically at the touch of his lips, small panting sobs torn from her throat as he moved upwards caressing the swelling flesh above the mole, his tongue tormenting the hardening nipple until she was ready to scream with frustration, the effort of lying completely still beneath the tantalising assault draining every last ounce of self-control, the sight of Kieron's dark head, where Nicky's had so often rested, sending slow waves of treacherous pleasure washing over her.

'Did his caresses arouse you?' Kieron muttered hoarsely. 'Or were you as cold with him as you are with me? I'm not cold, Briony, I'm burning up with wanting you. Can't you feel it?' He released her hands and placed one of them against the heated, damp flesh of his chest, groaning when her fingers trembled against his skin. His mouth fastened on her breast in possession and she was overwhelmed with an urge to stroke the dark hair, burying her fingers in its silky warmth, her flesh melting with the exquisite pain of his touch. He looked up at her suddenly, his skin flushed and damp, and it was too late to veil the betraying expression in her own eyes.

'Oh, God, Briony!'

His mouth burned against her, tasting every inch of her skin, his hands urging hers against his body as he shrugged out of his shirt and trousers, the hard warmth of his thigh, shadowed with dark, silky hairs, shockingly masculine as it forced hers to part.

The blood was drumming in her ears, her head thrown back against the pillows, her body shuddering convulsively as his lips grazed her throat, feathering tiny, tormenting kisses from jaw to lips which parted on a soft moan to plead his possession.

The first time she heard Nicky cry it didn't register, and it was only when Kieron went still that she realised what the sound was.

'Nicky,' she said in a voice that trembled unsteadily, completely unable to meet Kieron's eyes. What on earth had possessed her? She could think of no logical or valid excuse for her behaviour. It seemed that Kieron merely had to touch her to have her acting completely out of character.

'You'd better go to him,' he told her coolly. 'Weren't you lucky? Another few seconds and it would have been too late.'

She hated the way he lay watching her as she pulled on her robe, and keeping her back to him she said fiercely:

'Matt only came to talk to me. We didn't. . . .'

'You didn't what?' he jeered. 'Make love? Do you think I don't know that? You might be able to freeze out your mind, Briony, but your body is in revolt. It wanted me, even if you don't.'

'I'm not Gail!' she flung at him, sliding off the bed, crying with fear as his fingers fastened round her wrist, jerking her back.

'And just what does that mean?' he demanded dangerously.

'Exactly what you thought.' She refused to be intimidated. 'I rang the flat the other night and Gail answered.'

'And my puritan of a wife immediately leapt to the conclusion that because we were in the flat we must also be in bed. You couldn't be more wrong. Gail had come to see me about a problem she's been having at work, that's all.'

He released her smoothly, and Briony was sure she glimpsed satisfaction beneath the smile he gave her.

By the time she had comforted Nicky, who had been having a bad dream, Kieron was back downstairs, lounging in the kitchen as though nothing at all untoward had occurred.

'Fancy sunbathing?' he invited lazily. 'With your skin it might be as well if you got used to the sun a little in readiness.'

'In readiness for what?' Briony demanded sharply, annoyed with herself for letting him force her into a reaction.

'Didn't I tell you? That's why I've been working so hard lately, so that we can have a proper holiday.'

'I'm not going away with you,' she announced instantly. 'Go on your own, or take Gail with you.'

To her chagrin he shook with laughter.

'Oh, I don't think I could do that. You see, we're going to stay with my godmother, and I've already told her that my wife's a redhead. Of course, Nicky and I can always go alone.'

'You can't!'

'Try me,' he invited softly. 'Nicky and I are going whether you go or not. All the arrangements are made. I've booked the ferry. We leave next Wednesday.'

'*The ferry*? Where does your godmother live?'

'Oh, didn't I tell you? I must have had other things on my mind,' he taunted smoothly. 'She lives in France near St Jean Cap Ferrat. She has a small villa there with its own private beach. Nicky will love it.' There was a world of meaning in those last few words, and Briony knew that he intended to take

Nicky to France whether she went with them or not.

'Well, are you coming with us?'

'I'm certainly not letting you take Nicky on your own!'

'How gracefully you give in!' he mocked. 'Will you need to buy anything? I was going to suggest I arranged for Mrs Johnson to look after Nicky on Monday.'

'You think of everything, don't you?' Briony said savagely. There seemed to be no part of her life he hadn't taken over and she resented it bitterly. Not content with taking her son, he seemed to want to dominate her life as well.

'I try,' he agreed. 'Although I have been known to be defeated, if it brings you any comfort.'

With that enigmatic comment he strolled out into the garden, unbuttoning his shirt and dropping it carelessly on the lawn before stretching himself out in the sun. His torso was powerfully built and muscular, his stomach flat and taut. As she watched him awareness crept gradually over her and she had to turn away, trembling with fear at the discovery she had just made. She still loved him! Her body had known it long before her mind, hence its immediate reaction to him. But whatever happened he must never find out. That would be the crowning humiliation. She stuffed a fist in her mouth to prevent herself from screaming. Dear God, how was she to endure the rest of her life as his wife and yet still maintain the fiction that she hated him, especially if he continued in his present vein? She could never endure his full possession without betraying herself. Merely the thought of it turned her bones weak to the marrow with intense longing. What she must do was to maintain as great a distance between then as possible. She must never, never again allow a repetition of this afternoon's events. If Nicky had not cried when he did there could have been only one outcome, and her cheeks burned with shame as she recalled Kieron's mocking accusations to the same effect.

She went upstairs to wake Nicky, dressing him in a tee-shirt and shorts, his chubby brown limbs melting her heart with tenderness. When they got downstairs she sent him outside to Kieron, trying not to feel racked with envy and shut out as Kieron reached out a hand to encircle his son and pull him down beside him, the two dark heads achingly similar as Nicky curled up trustingly within the protection of his father's arm.

CHAPTER SEVEN

'WE'LL stop soon and have something to eat.'

Briony nodded. They were driving through Northern France, along a straight, fast road bordered with poplar trees, which seemed to go on for ever. Nicky had fallen asleep in his car seat and after the little boy's chatter had faded away a deep silence had filled the car.

Briony hadn't wanted to come away on this holiday. She could see no good coming out of it—and potentially a lot of danger. Since she had made the discovery that she was still in love with Kieron she had been filled with a terrible fear that somehow he might find out, and the effort of trying to appear cool and unaware of him had already seriously depleted her small reserves of self-control. It was as though after years of being subordinate to her mind, her body had finally thrown off its yoke, making its own needs and desires all too plain.

They had been driving since early morning and Briony was glad of the opportunity to stretch her legs when they eventually stopped for lunch in a small French town. Although she didn't want to admit it, it was a relief to let Kieron take charge, finding them somewhere to eat, and informing the waiter in crisp French that they would need something plain and simple for Nicky.

They were shown to a patio shaded by wisteria, its grey gnarled trunk and branches spread flat against the whitewashed wall of the restaurant, a small river flowing placidly on its way to the sea several yards away.

Briony even felt too tired to study the menu, and simply passed it over to Kieron with a listless shake of her head. 'You choose.'

He frowned and for a moment she thought she saw concern in his eyes. No doubt he was wondering how on earth he was going to cope with Nicky if she became ill, she thought sardonically. The little boy had been very good, but inevitably the long drive had bored and irritated him.

As she drank the cold soup Kieron had ordered she wondered what his godmother would be like. Kieron had said very little about her except that he always tried to spend some time each year with her, and that she was now a widow, and lived permanently in the South of France. Briony had visions of a lilac-coiffured dowager, immaculately made up and dressed in chic French clothes, and already she was dreading meeting her.

'Finish your soup,' Kieron instructed, breaking into her thoughts. She stared uncomprehendingly at him, unaware that she had pushed the bowl away barely touched. 'You're too thin,' he added. 'Héloise will have forty fits when she sees you.'

'Héloise?'

'My godmother's cook, maid, confidante, and friend,' he told her. 'They've been together since Tante Marian was first married.'

'I hope we're not going to be too much trouble.' Her forehead puckered as she thought of Nicky's noisy and demanding intrusion into the organised, restful world of two middle-aged ladies.

'We won't, unless Héloise accuses me of starving you,' he said dryly. 'And a little less of the martyred air might help, if you could possibly manage it.'

Briony finished her meal in silence. Kieron had the knack of making her feel like a sulky child, deliberately playing up to gain adult attention and sympathy. Even in the shadowed patio the sun was hot and she glanced automatically at Nicky's bare head. He had Kieron's skin colouring and took the sun well, but she had taken the precaution of buying him a couple of sun-hats, plus some thin long-sleeved tee-shirts just in case he was in danger of getting burned. Her own skin was more of a problem. Her long days in the cottage garden had given it a faint hint of colour, but it was liable to burn badly if she wasn't careful.

As though he had read her thoughts, Kieron said abruptly, 'Come and sit over here in the shade. You look pale, and I don't want you getting sunstroke.'

'I'm not a child,' she protested, but his eyes were scathing, the dark brows drawn upwards in disbelief as he glanced at her barely touched food.

'No? You deliberately drive yourself almost to the point of exhaustion; you refuse to eat properly, and then you sit outside in the full heat of the midday sun.'

'I shan't be ill,' she told him. 'I can't be. Who would look after Nicky?'

'Finish your lunch,' he told her abruptly. He looked angry, and Briony wondered if it was finally coming home to him exactly how taxing the responsibility of a child could be.

They drove all through the afternoon, stopping eventually in Avignon, where they were to spend the night.

Briony was too tired to appreciate the bustling town. Why was it, she wondered hazily, that simply sitting still all day doing nothing could be exhausting? She stole a look at Kieron, who was lifting Nicky out of the car. Although he had done all the driving it barely seemed to have affected him. His thin shirt clung to the powerful muscles of his back, the short sleeves revealing the bronzed forearms, the lean, male length of his legs moulded by close-fitting jeans. Briony was dressed very similarly, but whereas Kieron's shirt and jeans were moulded to a body undeniably male, Briony's snug-fitting cotton top and denims revealed softly feminine curves which drew more than one admiring pair of male eyes as they crossed the street in front of some *boules* players and entered the hotel.

Kieron had booked two rooms, at Briony's insistence. 'What are you afraid of?' he had taunted, and she dared not tell him it was herself. If they were to share a bed, no matter how platonically, she had no safeguard against herself turning unconsciously to Kieron during the night, and perhaps betraying herself completely.

Both rooms had double beds, and bathrooms, and she took Nicky into one of them, leaving Kieron in possession of the other. She had undressed Nicky before she realised that the overnight case she had packed for them was in Kieron's room, and having knocked on his door and received no answer, she assumed that he must have gone downstairs for something and pushed open the door.

The case was by the bed and she was just bending to pick it up when the bathroom door suddenly opened and Kieron emerged. His hair was damp and tousled, droplets of moisture clinging to his skin, and Briony felt herself flush darkly as she stared at his naked body. It seemed a lifetime before she could drag her eyes away. Her whole body felt weak and shaky, her mouth dry with tension, and it didn't help her composure one jot to hear Kieron laugh mockingly, his voice taunting as he drawled softly, 'Okay, you can look now without seeing anything that might shock your frigid little mind.'

He was wearing a brief towelling robe, but that didn't stop her imagination playing back to her exactly what was underneath it, and her body ached to touch his golden skin; to feel the powerful drive of his maleness against her. . . . She drew a ragged, shuddering breath, and pointed to the case.

'I came for this. . . .'

'What else?' he mocked. 'But let's get one thing

straight, Briony. When we get to my godmother's we shall be sharing the same room. As far as she's concerned, this is a normal, happy marriage, and that normality includes things like sharing a bedroom.'

She stared at him, appalled.

'But we can't!'

He shrugged dismissively. 'Why not? *I* never said anything about this marriage being in name only. It won't kill you.'

She thought of how she felt about him, and how impossible it would be to share his bed and appear indifferent, and said bitterly, 'Won't it?'

He reached for her, his thumbs stroking her throat, her body pressed against the damp warmth of his.

'We're married,' he said softly, 'and I don't intend to spend the rest of my life like a monk. Think of Nicky. Surely you aren't going to deprive him of the pleasure of brothers and sisters?'

Briony wavered, tormented against her will by the soft seduction he was weaving. It would be so easy to give in, to spread her fingers out against the hard warmth of his skin and give herself up to the thundering demand of her own body. Lost in indecision, she let Kieron tilt her head back and touch his lips to her throat in a coaxing caress, closing her eyes and letting herself be sucked down into a dark whirlpool of delight, her lips parting in heated anticipation.

'What are you doing with my mummy?'

Her eyes flew open and in other circumstances she would have laughed at the male belligerence in Nicky's voice as he frowned up at Kieron.

'You left me!' he accused Briony. 'You was gonned a long time.'

'Saved by the bell, but only this time,' Kieron

drawled in her ear. 'I can see I'm going to have to
invest in a bedroom door with a lock. 'Come on, I'll
carry you back to your room,' he told Nicky, bending
down to pick the child up.

'It isn't over,' he warned Briony. 'I meant what I
said.'

The farther south they drove the more arid the
landscape became, and Briony was conscious of a
nervous tension which wasn't entirely related to the
forthcoming meeting with Kieron's godmother. He
had made no further reference to last night, but she
did not doubt that he had meant exactly what he
said, and the worst thing was that part of her almost
wished that he would physically impose himself on
her and thus relieve her of the burden of making her
own decision, but she sensed that he was well aware
of how frail her barriers were and that he would use
time and propinquity as levers, waiting until she was
at her most vulnerable to make good his threats.

They drove through the hinterland of the Côte
d'Azur, thickly wooded with cypress, oak, ancient
scarred olive trees and the distinctive umbrella
pines; a slumbrous silence blanketed the countryside, luxurious villas were glimpsed here and there
behind wrought-iron gates.

In Nice the glitter and splendour of the Côte
d'Azur burst upon Briony's unprepared eyes in a
dazzle of unbelievable wealth, from the chrome on
the expensive cars which filled the city to the discreetly luxurious jewellery displayed on tanned,
seductive bodies.

'In Nice,' Kieron said dryly, 'all that glisters is
most definitely gold, solid and twenty-two carat.'

They took the corniche road from the city, winding along the flanks of the limestone cliffs of the pré-Alpes. Every time they swung round a bend Briony closed her eyes, only to open them again to drink in the view of the deep blue Mediterranean spread out below them.

Approximately twenty minutes after they left Nice they were driving through St Jean with its peaceful tranquillity and picturesque harbour.

Previously the nearest Nicky had ever been to the sea had been the lake in Regent's Park, and while the Channel crossing had left him relatively unimpressed, the sight of the harbour clustered with yachts had him round-eyed with excitement.

'Your godmother must be a very wealthy woman,' Briony murmured, unable to refrain from voicing her growing doubts. They were driving past luxurious villas set in the most beautiful countryside she had ever seen, and she was dreading the coming ordeal of meeting Kieron's godmother.

'Relatively so,' Kieron agreed. 'Her husband was a very prosperous businessman. He drowned with my parents in a sailing accident. Marian had stayed behind to look after me. I was twelve at the time, and I've never forgotten the look on her face when she broke the news to me. I'm afraid for a while I even blamed her for the accident. She had been the one to invite us all to stay with her, but she bore with me with the patience of a saint. Héloise took me on one side in the end and reminded me that I wasn't the only person who was suffering. When you share a tragedy like that with someone it forms a bond that can never be broken. Marian virtually took the place of my parents after that. I spent every

school holiday with her. You'll find she's a bit of a
romantic,' he added. 'Her happiness means a lot to
me, Briony. Don't disillusion her just to get back at
me. As far as she's concerned, we're a loving family
unit, and if you do anything to damage that illusion,
I'll make you suffer for it.'

They were turning in through wrought iron gates,
driving up to a house that made Briony catch her
breath in mingled delight and dismay. The villa
overlooked the sea on one side and Nice on the other,
its walls covered in ancient creepers and the windows
opened wide to the soft balmy air. A tall elegant
woman hurried gracefully down the steps fronting
the house as the car stopped, and although she was
undeniably beautifully dressed, there her resemblance to the creature of Briony's imaginings ceased
entirely. As Kieron uncoiled himself from the car,
she flung herself into his arms and studied him affec-
tionately, before hurrying round to Briony's side of
the car.

'My dear, I'm forgetting my manners!' she apologised warmly. 'Welcome to the Villa Jardin.' A slim
tanned arm indicated the beautifully kept gardens
which surrounded the villa, brilliant with oleander
and hibiscus, bougainvillea, flowering vividly against
the cream stone walls. 'And this must be Nicky!'

The little boy surveyed her rather doubtfully, and
Briony felt a lump come into her own throat as
Marian turned to Kieron and said unsteadily:

'Oh, my dear, he is *so* like you! Would you like to
come with me and have a nice cool drink?' she asked
Nicky casually. She was obviously accustomed to
children, Briony noted with surprised relief. She
made no attempt to overwhelm Nicky, waiting in-

stead while he looked at her rather thoughtfully
before announcing solemnly, 'Yes, please.'

'Oh, wait until Héloise sees you!' Marian said with
a smile. 'She's in the kitchen,' she told Kieron,
'making your favourite supper. I've given you the
Mimosa Suite. You'll be quite private,' she assured
Briony. 'It has a sitting room which opens straight
on to the gardens and from there there are steps
leading down to our private beach. It's rather rocky,
though, which is why we have the pool. And you
mustn't worry about Nicky. Héloise and I will be
delighted to look after him for you. Kieron tells me
that you haven't been well and that you're badly in
need of a rest. Of course you must be, you poor
child.' Kieron was taking the luggage out of the car
and Briony's eyes rested betrayingly on the tensed
muscles of his back.

'Kieron told me that you didn't have time for a
proper honeymoon,' Marian confounded her by
adding. 'I hope this holiday will make up for it. Now,
I must take Nicky to show Héloise. Although she
wouldn't admit it to a soul she has a terrible weakness for children, and she'll spoil him dreadfully.'

Briony followed her hostess through a cool tiled
hall which led off the arched patio and into an elegant drawing room decorated in peach and off-
white.

'You must be dying for a cup of tea,' Marian
declared sympathetically. 'I'll get Héloise to bring
us one while Kieron takes the luggage upstairs.'

Nicky was wandering round the room, staring
curiously at the elegant lamps and Chinese por-
celain, and Briony called to him not to touch anything.

The door opened and a woman Briony assumed to be Héloise walked in carrying a tea tray. She was built on solidly square lines, dark hair pulled back severely from an olive face, her eyes shrewdly assessing as they looked at Briony.

Marian introduced them, and Briony had the feeling that Héloise would not be slow to express disapproval of anyone who she thought might disturb her beloved mistress.

'And this is Nicky,' Marian announced, calling the little boy over.

This time when Héloise looked at her, Briony thought she glimpsed grudging approval in her eyes, although she was very surprised when Nicky willingly agreed to go to the kitchen with Héloise for a glass of orange juice.

'She has a magic touch with children,' Marian explained when they had gone. 'It is only with them that she truly relaxes her guard, and they seem to sense it. I can't tell you how happy I am about your marriage,' she added, pouring Briony a cup of tea. 'But Kieron is right. . . .'

'Aren't I always?' Kieron drawled from the door. He had changed into a clean shirt and close-fitting off-white jeans, and Briony's body trembled on a flood tide of love. 'But what specifically was I right about this time?'

'Briony,' Marian said with a smile. 'She does need a rest. I've told her she mustn't worry about Nicky, and if the two of you want to go out alone, he'll be quite safe with us. You must watch that skin of yours, though, my dear,' she warned Briony. 'My chemist does an excellent cream to prevent burning. I'm going to Nice tomorrow—which reminds me, I still haven't bought you a wedding present.'

'Just as well,' Kieron said easily. 'Until we find a permanent base we don't have anywhere to put anything. You might introduce Briony to French swimwear, though. My wife has a perfect figure and I object to seeing it clad in clothes that do it less than justice.'

Marian's face lit up.

'A shopping spree?—oh yes, I'd love that! It's a little late for a trousseau,' she laughed, 'but as this is practically your honeymoon I think we can stretch a point.'

'Really, there's no need,' Briony began, but the look of disappointment crossing the other woman's face, and the warning look in Kieron's eyes, forced her to change her mind and add unsteadily, 'But of course, if you're really sure you don't mind . . .?'

When she had finished her tea. Marian suggested that Kieron show Briony their rooms.

'Nicky will be quite safe with Héloise,' she forestalled. 'And if you'd like to rest for a while she'll look after him for you.'

Although the expensive luxury of the villa should have prepared her it was still a shock to discover that their 'rooms' encompassed a huge double bedroom complete with en-suite bathroom and an entire wall of mirrored wardrobes, with a dressing room off it, which Marian had thoughtfully organised as a bedroom for Nicky, plus a delightfully furnished sitting room overlooking Nice with its own small patio which led out to the swimming pool, and which as Marian had promised provided its own entrance to the villa.

'I'll have to have a word with Marian about

making sure the gate leading down to the rocks is childproof,' Kieron surprised Briony by saying as she stood by the window. 'Those steps are too steep for a small child and the rocks can be treacherous. Can he swim?'

Briony shook her head. She had taken Nicky a couple of times to the local baths, but lack of time had prevented her from going more regularly.

'Well, that can be something he can learn while we're here. Every child ought to before it's old enough to know fear.'

Cream and peach appeared to be the theme of the villa, Briony reflected as she unpacked, crossing acres of off-white, thick-pile carpet to put clothes away in the huge wardrobe. The bedspread and curtains had a Chinese motif of palest peach and green on a cream background, the theme repeated in the cream and black bathroom.

She paused as she stared at the bed. Tonight she would be sharing that with Kieron. She shivered inwardly.

'Why don't you rest before dinner?' the object of her thoughts suggested, walking into the bedroom from the sitting room. 'I want to go and have a chat with Aunt Marian.'

And presumably she wasn't wanted, Briony reflected bitterly.

She had a shower and lay down on the bed, having taken the precaution of locking the bedroom door. She only meant to rest for a few moments before dressing, enjoying the cool play of air against her skin, but somehow her eyes felt too heavily weighted to remain open, and it was so pleasant just to relax. She reached out for her robe, intending to pull it on, but was fast asleep before she even touched it.

A cold shaft of air across her back woke her, and in the dark shadows of the room it was several seconds before she remembered where she was.

She glanced at her watch in horror, unable to believe that she had slept so long. Kieron! Had he come looking for her and found the locked door? And Nicky! What on earth would Marian and Héloïse think of her? She rolled over frowning as the curtains billowed in the breeze from the opened French windows. She could not recall unfastening them, and her heart pounded unevenly as a figure detached itself from the shadows on the terrace and strolled towards her.

'So you're awake at last.'

Kieron! She reached feverishly for her robe, but he twitched it out of reach, his eyes mocking as he drawled softly, 'Oh no . . . you look much lovelier without. I thought the gods were indeed being generous when I came in here and found you lying so temptingly on my bed, like a sacrifice to Bacchus.'

'But I locked the door.'

'I know you did,' deep amusement tinged his voice, 'but you forgot about the patio, my lovely wife, and now, like Eve tempting Adam with the apple, you've aroused my appetite.'

She wriggled away from him, but he was too quick for her, his hands sliding over her skin to hold her waist while her heart beat so loudly she felt sure he must hear and correctly interpret its passionate demand.

'I told Aunt Marian you wouldn't want any dinner,' he murmured softly. 'Did you really not know that I would break down the door by sheer force once I'd glimpsed your delectable body? What a pity you've already had a shower.'

He laughed deep in his throat at her quivering reaction, stroking his fingers along her midriff and lowering himself on to the bed beside her. 'So timid and shy! I could almost believe you still a virgin if it wasn't for Nicky, and some particularly entrancing memories. Do you remember what you said to me then? How you pleaded so sweetly for me to possess your body, and how you cried with pleasure when I did?'

His hands were moving slowly upwards, moulding her breasts gently, moving lightly against her nipples.

'You do remember, don't you?' he breathed against her ear, his voice honey-sweet and seductive.

Briony tried to push him away, her palms tingling with shock as they came into contact with the male warmth of him.

'No!' She didn't know whether the word was a denial of his erotic words, or a denial of her own feelings, but Kieron seemed to be in no doubt. He rolled over, holding her clamped against him, his eyes hard as they searched her face.

'No?' he prompted softly. 'Then I shall just have to remind you. . . . The surroundings were similar, in that we were lying together on a bed. But then you pleaded with me to let you feel me against you without the restriction of our clothes!'

'No!' Briony denied desperately. 'I never said anything of the kind!'

'Perhaps not in so many words, but your body told mine pretty clearly that that was what you wanted. I even seem to remember you helping me out of my shirt. Like this,' he added huskily, sliding her hand against his chest where it tangled in the crisp dark hairs and clenched convulsively against him as he pulled his shirt free of his waistband and pulled her down against his naked warmth.

Her breasts swelled tautly with remembered warmth and Kieron groaned huskily deep in his throat. 'You see, you haven't forgotten at all,' he growled against her ear. 'You show me what comes next.'

For a brief moment she fantasised about doing just that, the palms of her hands sliding treacherously against Kieron's skin, the impeding jeans making her fingers curl resentfully as they ignored the commands of her brain to stop their sensual exploration and devote their energies to repulsing his masterful invasion of her senses.

'Still shy?' he teased, pinning her underneath him and raising himself up on one elbow to study the fluid lines of her body. 'I seem to remember much the same problem last time, although we eventually managed to overcome it. Undress me, Briony,' he urged against her ear. 'I love to feel you touching me.'

Her tongue flicked out to wet her dry lips, the betraying movement quickly stilled, but Kieron had seen it, and his hands cupped her face, and his own tongue lightly traced the outline of her mouth, his eyes gleaming in the darkness as she swallowed convulsively.

'Want me, sweetheart?'

Briony shook her head, not trusting herself to speak. Her whole body was trembling uncontrollably.

'Ah, that's better,' Kieron murmured. 'Now we're getting to the woman you've buried for so long. She wasn't cold and frigid, was she, Briony?'

Warning signals flashed despairingly in her brain, but her body was ignoring them, too languorous and aroused to heed their import. Her hands slid down to the hardness of Kieron's hips, tugging ineffectually at the cream cotton.

'Mmm, I know,' Kieron whispered, moving away slightly. 'That better?' he asked her seconds later, taking her hands and spreading them against the flat tautness of his stomach, his faint laugh lost on an unsteady groan as her fingers stroked tremulously against him, causing him to shudder deeply and fasten his mouth on hers in aroused demand.

There was a throbbing ache deep down inside her, a need for fulfilment that obliterated anything else. Her body arched provocatively against Kieron's, inciting him to subdue its subtle torment by inflicting his own revenge in the unhurried exploration of his mouth and hands. As though she had stepped from one world to another, leaving reality completely behind her, Briony responded passionately, her lips pressed feverishly against his skin, tasting its salty bitterness and feeling his gasped moan of pleasure. This time she was no uncertain novice having to be coaxed and taught, and her body remembered things her mind had long since refused to hold.

There was a moment when Kieron's thigh parted hers, when she felt spiralling panic and fought against him, but the rebellion was brief, her body already writhing heatedly even while her muscles contracted in protest.

'It's all right,' Kieron muttered thickly, caressing

her into relaxation, his 'Oh God, *Briony*!' lost in her own sharply passionate cry as her body welcomed him back with passionate sincerity.

She fell asleep still held in his arms, her body aching pleasurably, and her lips still curved in a slight smile.

When she woke up she was alone, and as realisation filtered through her mind sick panic clawed inside her. There was no sign of Kieron and somewhere deep inside her she had known that there would not be. Like the unreeling of an old film, pictures from the past flashed before her brain, memories of that other time filling her mind like the contents of Pandora's box. She was sitting up in bed, her arms locked tightly round her knees, rocking herself from side to side in mindless terror, when Kieron walked in.

'Briony.'

He tried to release her arms, but they were locked in place, her eyes burning with self-revulsion and pain as she stared at him.

'Did you think I'd left you?' he demanded comprehendingly. 'Oh, Briony . . . .' He made to take her in his arms, but she drew back, her eyes wild and bitter.

'Can't you leave me alone?'

A spasm of anger tightened his face.

'You weren't saying that a while ago,' he reminded her tautly. 'Far from it.'

Panic filled her. Another moment and he would have guessed how she felt about him. How he would deride her! How could any man who had made a marriage such as theirs be anything other than cynical about love?

'It was for Nicky's sake,' she flung at him. 'I don't want him to be an only child!'

For a moment she thought he was going to hit her. His face had gone white and almost ugly. 'My God, you mean you actually. . . . But of course it was for *Nicky*; whose needs are paramount, and for whose sake his mother so nobly sacrificed herself to my repulsive embrace and possession. I don't know whether to laugh or throw up,' he told her brutally.

'You were the one who said he needed a family,' Briony pointed out in a shaken voice. She had come too far to back down now. 'It was what you wanted too.'

'Was it? How the hell do you know what I wanted? You're incapable of knowing because you're incapable of human feelings. You wouldn't even begin to have the faintest idea about the needs which motivate real people. And to think I actually thought all that damned play-acting. . . .' He turned away abruptly. 'One day Nicky is going to grow up, and then what are you going to do with the rest of your life? Well, somewhere deep down inside that calculating little mind of yours lurks a real live woman, and I won't rest until I dig her out.'

'Why?'

'Why?' He watched her broodingly. 'Perhaps because you've just dealt me the biggest insult a woman can give a man, and my pride won't rest until I've held you in my arms and made you into a woman. Don't worry that I'm going to try tonight, though,' he added, surveying the large bed. 'My ego's taken just as much as it can for now. You really know how to emasculate a man, don't you, Briony? I'll sleep in

Nicky's bed for tonight, I don't think I could stand to share yours.'

What had she done? Briony thought numbly when he had gone. Oh God, what *had* she done? He wouldn't rest now until he had totally destroyed her, because that was what would happen if he carried out his threat. And she knew that he would.

As she lay sleepless in the huge bed she contemplated taking Nicky and leaving straight away, but Kieron had her passport, and besides, she had no money. If she could just survive this holiday, once they got back to England she would tell him that she wanted a divorce. She drifted off into nightmare-fractured sleep where a judge was calmly ordering that Nicky be chopped in half to be equally divided between his arguing parents.

CHAPTER EIGHT

THE shops in Nice drew awed gasps from Briony. Marian employed a taciturn, grizzled expatriate Scotsman to drive her car and care for the villa gardens, and he had taken them into the capital of the Maritime Alps.

Briony had already apologised profusely to her hostess for burdening her with Nicky and falling asleep, but Marian had swept her apologies aside with a charming smile, assuring Briony that she was not to worry.

'Héloise was thrilled, and Nicky is already the

apple of her eye,' she informed Briony, who had
observed the truth of this statement for herself at
breakfast.

Kieron had not put in an appearance at the table
on the sunny patio and when Marian mentioned that
he had gone swimming and was not likely to return
until after they had left, Briony felt able to relax
properly and enjoy her breakfast of croissants and
apricot preserve.

In fact Marian had been wrong, and he had
appeared just as they were leaving, his lean body
tanned and glowing with health, Nicky clinging ex-
citedly to his shoulders.

Kieron hadn't looked at Briony, and she had been
astounded when as they were getting in the car, he
had pulled her back against him, feathering a lazily
explorative kiss along the curve of her throat, before
turning her into his arms and kissing her properly.
But then she had remembered that Marian was
watching them and guessed that the embrace was
for her benefit. Unless—and she shivered to think
about it—he had already begun his hunt for the
woman he claimed she was concealing.

'What do you think of that bikini?' Marian asked,
drawing Briony's attention to a brief bandeau top of
emerald green silk and minute briefs that tied in
bows over the hips.

'It's outrageous,' Briony said frankly. 'And so is
the price.' Marian laughed. 'It'll suit you. Let's go
in and we can see how it looks on.'

It was useless for Briony to protest; Marian
intended to have her own way. The bikini was
purchased, despite Briony's scandalised protests, and
so were a pair of skimpy matching shorts and a soft

green and white striped toning tee-shirt.

'Have you brought anything special with you for evening?' Marian asked her later. 'Kieron is bound to take you to one of the casinos and although anything goes during the daytime, in the evening, especially in the casinos, high fashion is very much the order of things.'

Briony had packed a couple of cotton dresses, her swimwear, jeans, tee-shirts and one thin jacket for chilly evenings, but there had been no time to think further than that. However, she had no intention of allowing Marian to spend any more money on her and said so quite firmly.

The older woman's eyebrows rose.

'My dear, I'd love to spend some money on you— I have far too much of the stuff—but your husband seems to share your views and I have strict instructions that all the bills are to be handed to him and that you're not to be allowed to count the cost. His own words. I'm so happy for him, Briony,' she went on. 'There was a time when I thought I'd never see him smile again. You know, you aren't a bit as I imagined,' she added, going off at a tangent. 'Let him spend his money on you if it gives him pleasure. You're lucky, you know, so many husbands won't.'

Having elicited the information that Briony didn't have anything dressy with her, she took her to a small boutique in a shady courtyard filled with pots of geraniums tumbling over the grey stone in scarlet-orange splendour.

Madame was elegantly and chicly dressed in black. Marian said something to her in French and she clicked her tongue, assessing Briony with snapping black eyes.

'Well, *madame*,' she said at last in heavily accented English, 'do you wish to be *une grande madame*; *une coquette*, or *une fille bien élevée*—with such hair and eyes all are possible.'

'What she wants,' Marian interrupted, 'is a dress *très romantique*, for a husband from whom she has been parted for three years.'

Briony was just about to correct these misconceptions when the vendeuse rolled her eyes and said dryly,

'*Ma foi*, what you ask for is impossible! You wish to be all three!'

Marian laughed. 'And you will have the dress to enable her to do so, am I not right?'

The black eyes twinkled. 'Perhaps. Sit down, *madame*,' she instructed a bemused Briony, 'and I shall see what I can find.'

She was gone fifteen minutes, during which time Briony tried several times to question Marian about what she had said to her, but each time her nerve failed. And then, when they heard her footsteps returning to the salon, Marian said quietly, 'We shall talk later if you wish, Briony. I told myself before you arrived that I would accept you, for Kieron's sake, but I find already that I'm beginning to love you for your own, and I'm sure. . . .'

She broke off as the door opened, Briony's eyes widening appreciatively at the dress the vendeuse carried over her arm. In black paper taffeta, the full skirt billowed out over net petticoats and the top was little more than a brief backless shell, moulding her breasts.

'Try it on,' Marian urged her, watching her face. The taffeta rustled pleasantly against her skin, the stark colour emphasising her pale, creamy skin and the vivid intensity of her hair.

When she stepped rather hesitantly out of changing cubicle to show Marian, the older woman caught her breath in delight.

'Oh, my dear!' she exclaimed softly, 'you look quite ravishing!'

'If I may suggest an ebony comb studded with diamanté, to catch Madame's hair back so,' interposed the vendeuse, pulling back Briony's hair deftly. 'Or even satin flowers. . . ?'

The dress was boxed and they were on their way out of the boutique before Briony thought about the price.

Marian told her, chuckling at her stricken expression. 'My dear, it's a model and I'm sure it will be worth every penny in Kieron's eyes. Surely you're not frightened he'll be angry?'

It wasn't his anger that made her heart lodge uncomfortably in her throat, Briony admitted worriedly, but the thought of what conclusions he might draw when he saw her wearing the dress, that whispered seduction with every teasing rustle.

'I think I'll keep it as a surprise until we go out,' she said nervously to Marian, suspecting that the older woman might suggest a fashion show of their purchases when they returned to the villa. To judge from her disappointed expression Briony's suppositions had been correct, and her guilt at disappointing her kind hostess of this little treat was intensified when Marian insisted on buying Nicky a delightful lemon and white playsuit, which she told Briony defiantly was her present to him and was not going to be paid for by Kieron.

'You can't know how much seeing Nicky means to me,' she confided to Briony as they drove back to the villa. 'You see, Kieron is like the son I never had, and Nicky ... well, he's Kieron all over again and seeing him has revived many happy memories.'

'And unhappy ones, I'm afraid,' Briony said softly remembering what Kieron had told her about the death of his parents. 'Don't think me inquisitive, but have you never considered marrying again? You must only have been young when. ...' She bit her lip, fearing that she might be treading on sensitive ground, but Marian patted her hand and smiled.

'Don't worry, my dear, you aren't upsetting me. I was thirty-two when Gérard was drowned. We'd been married eight years and although we hadn't had the child we'd both longed for, our time together was so full of love and happiness that I could never bear the thought of another marriage. You see, Briony, when you've known true love, true happiness, you never want to replace it with counterfeit coin. The happiness I shared with Gérard has sustained me through the years of my widowhood. I have many pleasant friends, I have Kieron, and Héloïse, and now I have you and Nicky, so I still have happiness—it's just that it's a mellower version than that one shares with a lover.'

The first thing Briony saw when she climbed out of the car was Kieron's lean frame, sprawled out on a sun lounger by the side of the pool. The second was the curvaceous brunette bending over him and stroking suntan lotion into the smooth muscles of his back. Jealousy stabbed through her with white-hot knives, and she stood transfixed while Marian hurried past her, exclaiming in surprise, 'Louise, I thought you were in Paris?'

The brunette poured more oil on to Kieron's back, smoothing it in seductively.

'As you can see, Tante Marian, I'm not.' She shrugged petulantly. 'It was hot and I grew bored. Where, I thought, will be entertaining?—and then I remembered my Tante Marian.'

'And I thought I was the attraction,' Kieron mocked lazily, rolling over to shade his eyes from the sun and stare unblinkingly at Briony. Compared with the French girl in her minuscule scarlet bikini Briony felt overdressed and pallid. Her blouse was sticking uncomfortably to her back, her thin cotton skirt suddenly schoolgirlish and old-fashioned.

'Louise, come and meet Briony, Kieron's wife,' Marian instructed, and beneath the pleasant tones, Briony thought she caught a note of warning. Did Marian think that Louise might prove to be a tempting proposition which Kieron, man-like, might not be able to refuse, and that she, Briony, would be upset?

Even without Louise's proprietorial attitude towards Kieron, they could never have been friends, Briony decided. The French girl was one of those women who plainly despised her own sex, although her eyes did narrow fractionally when Kieron raised himself up on his elbows to study Briony's flushed face and enquire softly, 'I hope you carried out my instructions.'

'What is this, *chéri*?' Louise pounced acidly. 'What instructions did you give your wife?'

'That she buy herself a sexy bikini,' Kieron drawled, making Briony flush deeper.

Louise raised her eyebrows.

'The English are so stuffy about these things, unlike us French, although if I were married to such a man as you, I think I should dispense with the bikini altogether,' she finished provocatively.

Briony stiffened in outrage. Louise was flirting with Kieron right under her nose, and he, male that he was, was lapping it up. She glared at him with unguarded resentment, gasping when he turned to look at her his eyes narrowing with comprehension.

'Ah, but then you see, Louise, my wife knows that I enjoy discovering her beauty for myself, especially when it's temptingly packaged, with pretty wrappings and lots of bows,' he added thoughtfully, his eyes resting for a moment on Briony's slender hips almost as though he had already guessed what her packages concealed, and Briony's cheeks burned anew, as she made a vow never to wear the green bikini when her husband was around.

It came as a shock to discover that Louise was staying at the villa.

'It really is naughty of her to invite herself down here like this,' Marian complained to Briony over lunch. They were eating some deliciously fresh bread and home-made pâté, Nicky seated between them enjoying something a little less rich. Louise had persuaded Kieron to take her into Nice, claiming that she hadn't a rag to her back, and although Marian had suggested that François, the gardener and handyman, could take her, Louise had insisted provocatively that she wanted to go with Kieron.

'You won't mind lending me your husband for a while, will you?' she had pouted at Briony. 'After all, we are such close friends, and besides, Kieron tells me that you spend a lot of time with your little boy. Personally I find children extremely boring.'

Close friends! No doubt by that she meant lovers, Briony thought bitterly. Had Kieron been complaining to Louise that as a wife *she* left an awful lot to be desired?

As the heat of the sun started to increase, Briony took Nicky inside. He was telling her about how his daddy had taken him in the water and how he was teaching him to swim, and Briony listened halfheartedly with one ear while her mind tormented her with pictures of Kieron and Louise together.

When Nicky had gone to sleep she went to find Marian, but Héloise told her that the older woman usually rested in the afternoon.

'As that Louise knows,' she told Briony fiercely. 'And so you are here all alone while that she-cat takes your husband.'

'I don't mind,' Briony assured her unconvincingly. 'I think I shall go and sunbathe for a while. Louise's tan has made me feel quite envious.'

'Your skin is fair and you will burn if you are not careful,' Héloise warned her.

Bearing her advice in mind, Briony armed herself with some sun-screen and changed into a black swimsuit, picking up a towelling robe to cover her if she needed it.

She smoothed the cream into her arms and shoulders and lay back trying to relax.

The light touch of someone's hand on her shoulder roused her, and she stared sleepily up at Kieron.

'Where's Louise?' she asked, looking round for the French girl.

'Still shopping,' Kieron told her dryly. 'I'd had enough and I left her to it. She can phone for

François to pick her up when she's ready. I wanted to come back and see my beautiful wife.'

'Stop it!' Briony demanded fiercely. 'There's only the two of us here and you don't need to put on a show of being a devoted husband.'

His fingers were toying with the strap of her swimsuit and she pulled away in irritation, her eyes darkening stormily as he said curtly, 'What is this? Some relic from your schooldays? I thought I told you to get something new?'

'And if I don't choose to put myself on display like your "close friend" Louise, that's my affair.'

'We'll see about that!'

Before she could divine his intentions he had scopped her up, and carried her kicking and protesting to their bedroom, where he dropped her on the bed, and held her there with one powerful arm, while the other rummaged among the packages she had left on the bed, a cruel smile curling his mouth as he stared at the one holding the beachwear.

'Unless my memory is at fault we should find what I want in here. I think I can trust Tante Marian to carry out my instructions even if you won't.'

His low whistle of appreciation as he picked up the minute bikini brought Briony's rage to boiling point.

'What are you trying to do? Turn me into some cheap tart?'

She could have bitten out her tongue the moment she said the words, but instead of being angry, Kieron merely lifted his eyebrows sardonically. 'Oh, never cheap. And for your information, my dear wife, what I'm trying to do as you put it, is turn you into a warm, living, breathing, loving woman, who isn't ashamed of her sexuality, or my appreciation of it.'

His eyes flared smokily over her for a moment, and Briony shivered under his gaze, gasping as he pulled her to her feet, thrusting the bikini into her trembling hands and opening the bathroom door.

'You've got five minutes when I'll keep my back turned, but after that, if you aren't wearing that bikini, I'll put it on you myself, and enjoy doing so.'

It took her four, her fingers clumsy over the bows, and then when she was ready she shivered uncertainly in the cool bathroom, frightened to face Kieron in the brief, sexy costume.

'That's it,' he drawled unmercifully, stepping in through the door. 'Well, well!' His eyes roamed probingly over her slim body. 'It's even got the bows.'

'Don't you dare!' Briony gasped anxiously, stepping backwards, her eyes widening slightly.

She couldn't bring herself to look at her reflection as she stepped into the bedroom, already knowing full well how brief the bikini was.

She lay face down on a sunlounger, closing her eyes, and resolutely ignoring the rustling sound of Kieron's shirt and jeans being dropped on the paving beside her.

'Will you oil my back?' he asked.

She rolled over, mouth compressed. 'If you insist, although I doubt I'll be able to match Louise's skill.'

'Jealous?'

'Certainly not!' She poured oil into her palm and massaged it firmly into the tanned skin, trying not to react as the muscles relaxed beneath her touch.

'Umm ... now my legs,' Kieron murmured lazily.

She wanted to refuse, but instead she poured fresh oil, rubbing it in as though she would grind it into his bones. She knew that he was deliberately trying to make her aware of him, and—damn him—succeeding, but she was determined not to let it show.

'You can do the rest yourself,' she told him abruptly, straightening up and replacing the cap on the bottle.

When he swung himself off the lounger and dropped on his haunches beside her she froze, a frisson of awareness shivering over as he laughed softly deep in his throat.

'A little heavy-handed, but pleasurable none the less. And now, my lovely wife, it's your turn.'

Useless to object, so she didn't even try, forcing herself to lie still while his hands roamed enticingly over her skin, stroking in the thin sunscreen. Only once, when his fingers strayed close to the provocative bows fastening the minute briefs, did she move, but Kieron ignored her, his fingers sliding under the strings and tugging gently.

'Perhaps not here,' he murmured when she glared up at him. 'This must be a pleasure I shall reserve for later.'

'There won't be a later,' Briony gritted up at him. 'And will you please stop pawing me!'

'Pawing you?' His jaw jutted aggressively. 'By heaven, you try my patience at times, Briony, but this time I'll give you the benefit of the doubt and put it down to ignorance.'

'A lovers' quarrel?'

Neither of them had heard Louise approach. Her

look for Kieron was meltingly sweet, but her eyes
were cold as she glanced at Briony's slender body.

'Tonight you must take me to the casino, *chéri*,'
she purred to Kieron. 'I am feeling lucky. . . .'

'Then to the casino we shall go,' Kieron agreed.
'And we'll take Marian with us.'

Louise pouted.

'Tante Marian does not care for casinos.'

'And I think you'd better count me out,' Briony
said carelessly. 'There's Nicky. . . .'

'Who is quite happy with Héloise,' Kieron said
smoothly.

'Really, *chéri*,' Louise said crisply, 'English women
are so strange! I would not neglect my husband for a
small boy.'

'Not even when that small boy happened to be
your husband's child?' Briony said quietly and with
cold contempt. 'Please excuse me, both of you. Nicky
will be waking up, and I don't want him to wake up
alone. It can be very frightening.'

She thought for a moment that Kieron's eyes
darkened, but then his mouth suddenly twisted and
he looked away, ignoring her.

What was he trying to do? Show her how much
more of a 'woman' he thought Louise? She told
herself that she didn't care, but she did, achingly
so.

Briony dressed for the evening with scant enthusi-
asm, staring uncertainly at her reflection in the black
dress. She was just about to take it off when Kieron
walked into the bedroom.

'Don't tell me you chose that,' he demanded
grimly.

Her fingers faltered uncertainly against the silk flowers she had just tucked in her hair.

'Don't you like it?'

His eyebrows rose.

'What red-blooded male wouldn't?'

The brief, lightly boned bodice cupped her breasts, the black fabric stark against their swelling creaminess, her small waist emphasised by the full skirt.

'I was just going in to read to Nicky,' she said nervously as his eyes slid slowly over her.

'Lucky Nicky,' was his only comment, although he added laconically, 'Wait for me, I'll get changed and we can go in to dinner together.'

Nicky's eyes widened when he saw her, and Briony laughed as he sniffed appreciatively at her perfume. One day Nicky was going to be as potently male as his father, but for now he was still her precious little boy.

His eyes had just closed when Kieron walked into his room. He had changed into evening clothes, the narrow black trousers making him look taller and leaner, the white shirt and jacket a pale blur in the evening dusk. He kissed Nicky, who hugged him back sleepily.

Whatever else had not turned out right, at least Nicky had his father, and it was impossible to doubt their feelings for each other. Nicky's every other sentence seemed to contain the words 'Daddy said'. It would be easy to feel jealous, Briony admitted, but instead she could only feel relief that some good at least would come out of this ill-fated marriage.

Louise raised her eyebrows a little when she saw Briony, and there was jealousy in the narrowed gaze.

The brunette was wearing red—a slim satin sheath of a dress which emphasised her voluptuous curves.

Because they were going out, Héloïse had prepared a light meal. It was delicious, and Briony had consumed two glasses of wine before she realised that her glass had been refilled. They had been a mistake, she reflected a little woozily as they went out to the car.

Marian had insisted on Louise accompanying her in her car, leaving Briony and Kieron to follow alone.

As they drove down the Grande Corniche the city glittered beneath them, the dark blue Mediterranean bristling with expensive yachts, bedecked with coloured lights.

Kieron parked by the harbour and they walked past the glittering array of craft before turning away from the coast, placing Briony's arm through his as he drew her across the road. The slight contact triggered off insane desires which she fought hard to quell.

The casino was noisy and full, and Briony watched the tables, wide-eyed and awed that anyone could lose money with such careless sangfroid.

Louise smiled at her condescendingly. They had been waiting for them in the foyer, and no sooner had they all stepped into the main gaming room than Marian had been swept off by a party of old friends, delighted to see her and anxious for her to spend some time with them.

'You will dance with me, won't you?' Louise pleaded with Kieron. 'We always used to dance so well together . . . as we did everything. . . .'

'But now I'm a married man and must dance only with my wife,' Kieron said dryly.

He bought some chips and handed some to Briony. She followed his instructions carefully, but in no time at all the small pile had disappeared.

'You are no gambler,' Louise said scornfully. 'You should have placed the lot on one number.'

'Briony's too cautious to be an all or nothing girl.' Kieron's mocking smile pierced her heart. 'But I'm trying to teach her.'

Louise wanted a drink, and as Kieron turned to summon a waiter, they were parted by the crowd. A feeling of panic came over Briony as she searched anxiously for him, and the crowd seemed to press down upon her until she felt that she was suffocating. At last it parted and she saw Kieron standing with his back to her, Louise in his arms.

When she reached them the brunette's smile was smug. 'I nearly fell over and Kieron had to rescue me. Which he did most gallantly,' she added, kissing Kieron lingeringly on the mouth.

Something exploded inside Briony. She had nearly been crushed to death by the crowds, but all that Kieron had been concerned about was rescuing Louise from 'nearly falling'.

'It's stuffy in here,' she said coldly. 'I'm going to get some fresh air. I'll meet you by the car when you're ready to leave, Kieron.'

She hurried out before either of them could speak. Let Kieron have Louise if that was what he wanted. She didn't care. Let them dance together and make love together. Let them. . . . She dashed away the angry tears with the back of her hand, stumbling out into the fresh air and heading instinctively for the sea. She had just crossed the road when Kieron's fingers clamped on her arm.

'What the hell was all that about?' he demanded savagely. 'You little fool, you didn't even look when you crossed the road back there!'

'Perhaps I'm tired of looking,' Briony said fiercely. 'Especially at you and Louise. Oh, why don't you go back to her? I'm sure she's far more satisfactory than I am in every way.'

'Except that she doesn't happen to have borne my son,' Kieron said softly.

'Which is the only reason that we're married, and I wish to God you'd remember that and stop tormenting me with this fictitious "lovemaking". If that's what you want, get it from Louise—I'm sure she would be more than happy to oblige.'

'I'm sure she would, but you see I've set myself this goal, and I'm not giving up until I reach it.'

They had reached the car, and Kieron unlocked it. Briony climbed in, ignoring him and yanking her seat belt across her body.

The steep road climbed out of the town, the sea left far below. The road was deserted and Kieron stopped the car.

'What are you doing?' Briony demanded icily as he reached towards her, but the words were smothered against his jacket, his voice very dry as he murmured enigmatically, 'Just putting into practice a little theory.'

Her lips parted in anger, trembling as they felt the hard pressure of his, his tongue coaxing them apart so that he could savour the full inner sweetness. Something had happened to her self-control. That scene in the casino had left her vulnerable and unguarded, and she longed to bury her fingers in the thick darkness of his hair and beg him to take her to a place where nothing existed but themselves and no conscience could intrude with unwanted reminders that he didn't love her.

The kiss deepened and she sighed, suddenly pushing him away as she remembered how he had held Louise.

He let her go and switched on the engine, his face unreadable in the heavy dusk. Was that disappointment shafting through her so fiercely? She refused to think about it. It was degrading to want the lovemaking of a man who was merely slaking a desire—and obviously not a very strong desire at that, or had Louise's arrival already slaked it?

She was barely aware of the grandeur of their surroundings. They were going back to the villa alone, and now, when it was too late, she regretted that they had not waited for the others. Kieron was merely playing with her, she was sure of that, but might he not make good his earlier threats anyway, merely as a form of punishment for her defiance. Last night after their lovemaking she had drifted immediately into relaxing sleep, but tonight, lying by his side, aware of him in every nerve, would she be able to do the same?

CHAPTER NINE

WHEN they went into the villa the telephone was ringing. Kieron picked it up and from the brief conversation Briony deduced that Louise was on the other end of the line. This was confirmed when Kieron hung up.

'Louise wants me to go and pick her up,' he said tersely. 'I shouldn't be long.'

Briony shrugged, hoping he wouldn't see the jealousy she felt. 'Take as long as you like, I don't care.'

She heard the car drive away when she was in the bedroom, and only then would she admit how much she had hoped he would refuse to go, and yet if he had they would have been alone together in these impossibly romantic surroundings. She stayed by the window for a long time staring out into the velvet darkness of the night, and then Nicky murmured something in his sleep, reminding her of exactly why she was here as Kieron's wife.

It was late when she heard him come in. She pulled the covers up round her head, forcing herself to breathe as though she actually were asleep, drawing herself as far away from Kieron's side of the bed as possible.

She heard him moving about the bedroom, whistling slightly under his breath, her ears stretched for every single sound. It seemed an eternity before the shower was turned off and he re-emerged into the bedroom, and then the covers were twitched back, the bed depressing as he got in. She longed to turn her head and see what he was doing, but if she did he would know that she wasn't asleep. Her throat ached with tension and as he turned over, brushing against her back she stiffened slightly, trying not to tremble.

If it hadn't been for Marian, of whom he was so fond and whom he wouldn't want to shock or hurt, would he have been sharing Louise's bed tonight?

He moved again and she froze, her eyes opening wide with shock as he mocked softly, 'Goodnight,

Briony—sweet dreams.'

He had known all along that she wasn't asleep! Her fingers curled into two small impotent fists. Why had he let her go on pretending like that, making a fool of herself, when all the time. . . . Her angry thoughts chased this way and that as she dwelt on various means of exacting revenge, until she realised from the deep, even breathing at her side that Kieron had bested her yet again, and was fast asleep while she was forced to lie wide awake at his side, tormented by visions of him with Louise held tightly in his arms. No doubt if he had been sharing a bed with *her* they wouldn't have been sleeping with half the width of it between them.

She woke during the false dawn, wrapped in a delicious warmth, a sound like the sea in a shell pounding comfortingly against her ear, and as she wriggled languorously it was several seconds before she realised that the sound was Kieron's heartbeat and that some time during the night she must have turned towards him and crept into the warmth of the arms that were closed tightly around her, one lean hand possessively cupping her breast. Kieron was fast asleep, dark stubble shadowing his jaw. Briony tried to move away, but his arms tightened at once, and terrified that he might wake up and find out what she had done, Briony forced herself to relax, unaware of the faint smile flickering across Kieron's mouth as she drifted back to sleep.

The next time she awoke, it was to the piercing sound of Nicky calling her name. She opened her eyes drowsily and saw that the little boy was sitting on the bed next to her, his eyes reproachful.

'I thought you was never going to wake up. My

daddy's going to teach me to swim, and I want my breakfast.'

Briony opened both eyes in response to this wholly male demand, tempted to tell Nicky that breakfast would have to wait.

'Mummy won't wake up,' she heard Nicky saying solemnly, and then before she could protest, the covers were twitched back by a tanned male hand and Kieron was standing in front of her dressed in jeans and a thin cotton shirt unbuttoned to the waist, his eyes laughing as he surveyed her sleepy, tousled indignation.

'Come on, lazybones,' he grinned. 'Nicky and I have been up for ages, haven't we, old son?'

Nicky nodded. 'Daddy had to dress me,' he told Briony accusingly.

Briony glanced at her watch. Half past seven. 'Poor Daddy,' she said tartly.

Kieron leaned over the bed, his eyes wicked as he whispered, 'He'll dress you as well, if you ask him nicely.'

She shot off the bed, furious as his laughter followed her about the room as she hurriedly found clean underwear, a brief top and shorts.

'Don't be long, Mummy, 'cos we've got a surprise for you,' Nicky instructed as she disappeared in the bathroom. 'Can I bounce on this bed?' she heard him asking Kieron as she stepped into the shower. It gave her a faint pang to think of Kieron washing and dressing his son while she slept unaware.

The bedroom was empty when she emerged from the shower. She made the bed quickly, going into Nicky's room to tidy up his things. Héloïse had told her that she was not to worry about such things and

that she was at the villa for a holiday, but sheer
force of habit had her doing the small tasks without
really thinking. Already her skin had taken on faint
colour—more a soft apricot glow than a tan, but her
skin seemed to have a bloom it had lacked for too
long, and as she sat down to brush her hair and
apply a faint touch of make-up she was disturbed to
see how her eyes glowed so softly. She had all the
unmistakable signs of a woman deeply in love, and if
she wasn't careful Kieron was going to see them and
put two and two together.

When she walked out on to the patio, the others
were already there, Nicky's face bursting with excitement and impatience.

'Can I do it now?' he asked Kieron.

Kieron nodded his head, and just as Briony started to
frown uncomprehendingly, Nicky burst out, 'Happy
birthday, Mummy, come and see what I gotted you!'

Her birthday! She realised with a start that with
their marriage and then this holiday, she had completely forgotten the date. Nicky was beaming with
excitement, and for the first time she noticed the
small pile of presents by her plate. A huge lump rose
in her throat. It had been so long since anyone remembered the occasion. Kieron had got up and was
walking towards her, and she swallowed the betraying tears. Marian was smiling at her understand-
ingly, and for once she felt no inclination to shrink
away as Kieron took her hand, lacing his fingers with
hers. As she looked up at him she knew he had been
responsible for the surprise, a legacy of those long,
long, hot summer days they had shared, when her
birthday had been something they had celebrated
with champagne and he had bought her pink roses

and perfume. Even so she was surprised that he had remembered.

'Open mine first, Mummy,' Nicky demanded 'It's that one.' He pointed to a small flat package wrapped in pretty pink paper and tied with silver bows.

It was a silk scarf printed in shades of green, so beautiful and sophisticated that Briony knew Nicky alone had not been responsible for its purchase.

'Daddy and I went and boughted it,' Nicky said importantly. 'Do you like it?'

'I love it,' Briony assured him, dropping a kiss on his head.

There were cards from Héloise and François and a huge bottle of her favourite perfume from Marian, as well as a silver-framed photograph of Nicky.

'Oh, you shouldn't have,' she protested impusively, kissing the older woman warmly. 'But thank you very much. Where's Louise, by the way?' she asked lightly, determined not to betray any awareness of the fact that there was no gift from Kieron. Of course there was no reason why Kieron *should* buy her anything, just the opposite!

'Louise is still in bed,' Marian announced, breaking in upon these unhappy thoughts. 'But, Kieron, haven't you bought Briony anything?'

Briony longed for the question to have remained unasked, but then of course, as far as Marian was concerned, their marriage was perfectly normal, and she would expected Kieron to have bought his wife something.

'Yes, I have,' Kieron astounded her by drawling, his eyes amused as they rested fleetingly on her startled face. 'But to spare her blushes I thought it might be better if I gave it to her when we're alone.

In fact,' he added, getting up from the table, 'I was going to ask if you would keep an eye on Nicky for us while I did.'

Marian laughed, and told him he was making Briony blush.

'I know,' was his wicked response. 'I like it.'

There was no way Briony was going to get out of going with him, and with a rather forced smile she thanked Marian for looking after Nicky and got up to follow Kieron.

When he opened the french windows to their sitting room, she hesitated, and he watched her through narrowed eyes.

'Scared?' he taunted softly. 'My gift isn't anything physical, although you're on the right lines. I'm hoping it will help that long-buried woman in you to surface. Here you are.'

He threw her a large oblong parcel wrapped in soft green tissue paper and tied with matching ribbons.

Confused, Briony caught it, fingering the paper doubtfully.

'Open it,' Kieron demanded softly. 'Marian isn't going to rest until she finds out what it is. You really are the most exasperating female,' he added, when she made no move to open the parcel. 'Any other woman would be consumed with curiosity.'

Realising that she wasn't going to be allowed to escape until it was open, Briony hesitated over the wrappings. The name on the box when the paper was removed drew her brows together in a slight frown, but this was nothing to the expression on her face when the lid was removed and the contents of the box presented themselves to her startled eyes. Her fingers trembled over a dainty bra in peach satin trimmed with écru lace; matching panties so brief as to be almost indecent, a tiny, cobwebby suspender belt, and sheer silk stockings. There was also a nightdress in gossamer-fine silk and a matching negligee, but these she barely took in, her face going white and then a dull, dark red, as she stared at the silk and satin underwear.

'How dare you buy me anything like this?' she demanded at last in a voice which shook with rage. 'How dare you!'

'I wanted to remind you that you were female,' Kieron drawled. He was standing watching her, his hands in the pockets of his jeans, his manner outwardly relaxed, but she sensed within him a waiting, assessing quality which added churning sickness to her other emotions. 'Or perhaps it was just to remind myself,' he said coldly, his eyes suddenly darkening as she flung the box down on the bed. 'There's precious little other evidence.'

Quite why she should be so infuriated with the gift, Briony did not know. Perhaps it had something to do with the fact that since Nicky's birth there had never been money to spare for such luxurious items; her underwear had all been chain store purchased and bought to last; there hadn't been the opportunity or the need to think of herself in feminine terms, and the sight of those feminine, frivolous pieces of satin and lace touched the deep aching chord inside her which had once thought only of dressing to please Kieron and which had slowly and silently died when he left.

'Get out of here,' she breathed quietly. 'There's no woman to be disinterred, Kieron, you destroyed her completely.' She had her back to him and when she turned round the room was empty. Like a sleep-walker she crossed to the bed, touching the satin absently, folding the minute garments and putting them back in the box. It was a gift more suitable for the Louises of this world than for her. She opened a drawer and pushed the box as far into it as it would go, and then, holding herself erect, she went back to the patio.

'Are you all right, Briony?' Marian asked in concern. 'You look pale.'

'I'm fine. Where's Nicky?' She looked round for the little boy.

'Oh, Louise wanted to go into Nice, so Kieron has taken her, and Nicky went with them.' She frowned a little. 'I'm sorry about Louise descending on us like this. Her mother is an old friend of mine, but Louise has never been one of my favourite people.'

'She does seem a bit of a man-eater,' Briony commented dryly, guessing what was worrying her hostess. 'Am I right in thinking that she and Kieron had a bit of a thing together at one time?'

Marian's smile was relieved.

'How sensible you are, my dear! I thought you might be worried about Louise's rather obvious tactics. I'm sure Kieron never felt more than a casual interest in her. It was the summer after he was so ill, and I'm afraid I rather encouraged her at the time. I was desperate for something to lift him out of himself. Those were dreadful times. I'm afraid I was rather bitter about you in those days, Briony. In fact you are far different from how I imagined you would be.'

'You were bitter about me?' Briony queried with a frown. 'I'm afraid I don't understand.'

Marian looked a little flustered.

'Oh, my dear, I don't want to re-open old wounds, but when Kieron came back from Africa and was so ill, I was sure you would have second thoughts. You see, he'd already told me about your first letter, but I persuaded him to write again. I was so sure you would relent. He told me what had happened, but when his second letter was returned without a word—well, I'm afraid I came very near to hating you.' She broke off to stare at Briony's white face. 'Oh, my dear, I'm so sorry! I shouldn't have mentioned it. Kieron warned me not to. . . .'

'I'm very glad you did,' Briony said in a shaky voice, 'because you see, I've never written to Kieron in my life. Not when he walked out on me, leaving me to face the Press, and not even when I knew I was expecting Nicky, and everyone seemed to have turned against me. I vowed I never would. He'd made it plain that he wanted nothing more to do with me. . . .'

'Nothing more to do with you? Briony, you're quite wrong,' Marian interrupted in shocked anger. 'Why, when he came back from Africa, all through his illness all he thought of and spoke about was you. I never thought he would pull through, you know, and writing to you was my last hope. I thought that once he'd seen you, heard your voice, he would try to get better. It was almost as though he had a death wish, but his body defeated him, recovering against his will.'

'Please . . .' Briony demanded in a tremulous voice, 'what are you talking about? Kieron left me after searching my flat for the evidence he needed for the Myers story, and I never saw him again. I woke up that morning . . .' she broke off, blushing slightly, and then added bravely, '—expecting to find myself in his arms, instead of which I was completely alone. By the end of that day Kieron's story was all over the papers and I was being interviewed by the police concerning my part in the Myers affair.'

Marian sighed. 'Oh, my dear, I'm so sorry. I understand why you should feel so bitter.'

'I waited for him to get in touch with me,' Briony continued as though she had not spoken. 'All through the court case I went on hoping, right up until Nicky's birth, but there was nothing ... nothing at all.'

'Oh, my poor child!' Marian said with compassion. 'How could he contact you? Before the story broke he was contacted by the paper and ordered to take over from their war correspondent in Angola, who'd been shot and seriously wounded. He begged them for time—time to explain to you why he hadn't been able to tell you about the Myers story, but they were adamant. Only a few planes were being allowed in and out of Angola and he had to be on the one leaving that morning.'

'But surely he could have done something before he left? A note. . . .'

Marian's eyes were puzzled. 'But he did. He told me so himself, although very grudgingly. Kieron isn't a man to confide his private hopes and fears freely to others, however close. He wrote to you begging you to trust him and have faith, saying he would explain as soon as he returned.'

'I never got the letter,' Briony said slowly, trying to remember the exact sequence of events on that dreadful morning. Had there been any letters that morning? There were some, for Susan, and she had left them in the kitchen. They had gone when she returned and one of her neighbours had told her with relish of how the police had arrived while Susan was in the flat and how the other girl had left with them. Susan! The blood left her face. What if Kieron's letter had been delivered during the morning and Susan had opened it? Bitter and resentful, might she not have destroyed or withheld it as a means of getting back at the girl who had in all innocence been the means of her brother's downfall?

'You've thought of something?' Marian declared shrewdly.

'My flatmate, the girl whose brother was convicted—she returned to the flat that day.'

'And she could have misappropriated the note and replied to it? But of course! Kieron did say he left instructions for it to be delivered by hand.'

'But that doesn't explain why he made no attempt to contact me afterwards,' Briony persisted. 'Surely. . . .'

'Briony, he couldn't,' Marian said gently. 'When he was in Angola he was taken prisoner and he was in gaol for six months. Eventually he managed to escape and make his way to the border where he was found in a delirious state. It was six weeks before he was well enough to leave hospital. He was as thin as a skeleton and had contacted a very debilitating fever. At one stage he even seemed to have lost his memory, and it wasn't until he came to me to re-cuperate that I learned what had happened between the two of you. Oh, he didn't *tell* me,' she added when Briony looked surprised. 'I told you, he had the most dreadful fever, and he was delirious. It didn't take the intelligence of a genius to work out that the 'Beth' he called for so continuously was very, very important to him. When he had recovered enough I taxed him with it, and the whole story came out. He was very bitter about the whole thing. He'd wanted the paper to delay the story and give him time to tell you himself, but they were afraid that if they didn't print it straightaway, someone else would. For a long time I honestly thought he was going to die. He made no effort to recover, and then at last, in desperation, I coaxed him into giving me your name and address, and I wrote to you begging you to get in touch with us. When the letter was returned unopened it seemed to change something in him. He became much harder, and then Louise came to stay with me, and she made him laugh, and I knew he was going to live.'

A jumble of emotions held Briony still.

'I moved,' she said in a low voice. 'I had to change my name because of the publicity, and I let the flat go. I bought a house, for Nicky. . . .' Tears welled and splashed down on to the table, and then suddenly she was crying as she hadn't cried in years, and Marian was comforting her as though she were Nicky's age.

'I think this calls for a cup of tea,' she said firmly, when at last the flow had stopped.

Briony responded with a weak smile. 'The universal panacea!' She wondered if Marian thought it strange that Kieron had said nothing of all this to her himself, and then realised from the shrewd look Marian was giving her that the older woman hadn't been entirely taken in by their deception.

'You do love him, don't you?' she asked softly.

Briony managed a watery smile. 'What would you say if I said "no"?'

'Call you a liar,' Marian retorted frankly. Then she smiled. 'Because it's your birthday, Héloise is preparing a very special meal for tonight. It's always easy to give advice, Briony, and always hard to take it. Despite the magnificent efforts you've both made to hide it, I can tell that things aren't entirely as they should be between you and Kieron. He's a man with considerable pride and I suspect finds it difficult to lay his head on the block a second time. Find a way of showing him how you feel, and I'm sure you'll find he will meet you half way. You already have the deepest bond that human beings can have— Nicky,' she explained gently, when Briony looked puzzled. 'You bore Kieron's child even when you thought he'd deserted you, and you love him. Let that be your stepping stone across the river that divides you.'

Marian's revelations kept Briony's thoughts busy for the rest of the day. When Kieron and Louise returned from Nice she watched Kieron teaching Nicky to swim in the pool, Louise's pouting face showing how much the other girl resented Kieron's attentions to his child.

'Let's go out for dinner tonight,' she suggested, with a kittenish yawn as she stretched out full length in a minute white bikini, placing herself strategically where Kieron couldn't help but notice the smooth golden curves.

'It's Briony's birthday, and Héloise is making something special to mark the occasion,' Marian said pleasantly but firmly. 'But if you want to go out, Louise, don't let us stop you.'

For a moment resentment flashed in the other girl's eyes, but then she shrugged disdainfully.

'So, it is your name day,' she said speculatively to Briony. 'Did Kieron buy you a gift?'

The suspicion she had been harbouring that Louise had been responsible for the purchase of the underwear died instantly, to be replaced by a small imp of mischief.

'Mmm ... I think I'll wear it tonight,' she murmured idly.

Louise looked puzzled, and Kieron showed no sign of having overheard. But Marian's revelations had given Briony the courage to do things she would not have contemplated before, and if revealing the woman she had once been was the way to re-awaken the love which had once blazed between them, then she was more than prepared to do so.

'Look, Mummy, I'm swimming!' Nicky shrieked, splashing enthusiastically at the water, while Kieron supported him.

'Lovely, darling,' Briony smiled appreciatively, mentally reviewing her wardrobe. She couldn't wear the black dress again, and yet she had nothing else suitable for a celebratory dinner.

'I wonder if I could borrow François and go into Nice?' she asked Marian apologetically. 'Birthdays haven't come very high on my list of priorities recently, and I haven't anything to wear.'

Marian burst out laughing. 'Quite a change from the girl who announced she didn't need anything yesterday!' she teased. 'Of course you may, my dear. Would you mind if I came with you?'

This time Briony studied the boutiques closely. She knew what she wanted, and Marian glanced at her in surprise as she examined and discarded several dresses.

'What exactly are we looking for?' she enquired curiously.

Briony smiled wryly 'Something I can wear over satin and lace underwear.'

For a moment Marian's eyes widened in perplexed surprised and then she laughed. 'Oh, I see—the mysterious birthday present. Look, I know somewhere that specialises in silk separates. Let's try there.'

Half an hour later they returned to the car, both feeling very satisfied with themselves. The boutique had proved to have exactly what Briony wanted—a softly shaped silk skirt in palest peach teamed with a matching blouse in silk, but embroidered like broderie anglaise, sleeveless and cut low over her breasts, edged with a tiny provocative frill and fastening down the front with tiny pearl buttons. She had also bought a pair of ridiculously spindly-heeled sandals to match, which for all their outrageous price were little more than a high heel and several slim strands of plaited leather across the toes.

'Just right for sheer stockings,' Briony commented impishly to Marian as she paid for them, and after a startled glance the older woman had replied thoughtfully, 'I'm beginning to see what Kieron means when he talks about the woman you've buried away, although now she seems to be re-emerging with a vengeance!'

Briony purposefully waited until Kieron was ready himself before changing for dinner, and she was aided in this unknowingly by Marian, who suddenly remembered that such a celebration demanded something special to drink and asked Kieron to go out and get it.

'Champagne, of course,' Briony heard her saying as Kieron followed her out of their sitting room, 'and I understand Héloise is giving us duck with orange for the main course.'

When he had gone, Briony had a leisurely bath, soaking herself in her favourite bath oil, her hair tied up in a knot to keep it dry.

When she emerged from the perfumed water she dried herself and sprayed her body liberally with a perfumed emollient. What had Kieron called her the other night—'a sacrifice to Bacchus?' Her hands trembled on the satin underwear. Never, ever in her life had she set out to deliberately entice a man as she was doing tonight, and for that reason alone she simply dared not think of failure. Her colour was high as she caught sight of herself in the sheer stockings and cobwebby lace. She was just reaching for her blouse when the door suddenly opened and Kieron strode in, stopping dead as he saw her. For a second his eyes widened in entirely male appreciation and then he was smiling, no emotion discernible in his expression but satisfied comprehension as he drawled mockingly.

'So I was right after all.' His fingers ran lightly along one silk-clad thigh and Briony's flesh trembled in response. 'What wrought the change, I wonder?' Before Briony could tell him, he had turned away, leaving her breathless and faintly disappointed. 'I'll go in and have a look at Nicky while you finish dressing. Unless of course you want any assistance?' One dark eyebrow rose sardonically, and Briony longed more than she had longed for anything in her life for the sangfroid to say casually, 'Yes, please. . . .' But she still lacked the courage for such responses, and although her eyes appealed for help,

Kieron was already walking towards Nicky's room, leaving her no alternative but to pull on the peach silk blouse and fasten it with fingers which had suddenly become terribly clumsy.

The faintest touch of green eyeshadow and a slick of lip-gloss were all the make-up she needed. The peach silk whispered softly round her legs, and she wondered if it was merely the sensuous feel of the rich fabric against her flesh that made her feel such wanton desire for the touch of Kieron's hands, and the demanding possession of his body.

Louise scowled when she appeared in the elegant dining room, her eyes flashing resentfully over the peach silk and the rounded curves of Briony's breasts beneath the low neckline. She was wearing another slim sheath of a dress, but the black fabric made her skin look faintly sallow and Briony knew without vanity that tonight, of the two of them, she looked the more attractive.

They started the meal with a fresh fruit cocktail, deliciously refreshing and light before the succulent roast duckling with its sharp orange sauce and crisp vegetables cooked and served as only the French seemed to know how.

She sipped her dry white wine, enjoying the way it set her blood on fire, a faint flush on her cheeks as she caught Kieron's eye across the table.

To follow the duckling they had crêpes suzettes and fresh, sweet strawberries, and although Briony shook her head, Kieron insisted on pouring her a glass of Sauternes, gold and honeyed and tasting like nectar.

By the time the meal was over she felt lightheaded. Marian suggested that they adjourn to the drawing-room, where she drew Louise into conversation about her mother, much to the latter's obvious annoyance.

Briony touched her tongue to her upper lip, wishing Kieron would stop staring out into the darkness and come and sit beside her. He was wearing evening clothes again and they made him seem slightly remote.

'I think I'll go to bed,' Briony said breathlessly at last, hoping no one would notice her faint hesitation. It was only ten o'clock, but surely Kieron would. . . . She glanced hesitantly at him, willing him to turn round and announce that he would go with her, but he did not, and she felt Marian's eyes resting sympathetically on her, as she turned to leave the room.

In their bedroom she sat on the edge of the bed, plucking nervously at the bedspread, and starting at every tiny sound, her eyes fastened on the door. Half an hour passed with no sign of Kieron, and her hopes started to fade, her earlier excitement turning to misery. Either she had not made her invitation plain enough or he was not interested enough to take it up. She waited another fifteen minutes and then walked out of the house, past the floodlit pool, to where the narrow steps led down to the beach. The pounding of the sea against the rocks was primeval and eternal. The evening was warm, a soft breeze blowing inland, and possessed by an urge she could barely comprehend, Briony slowly removed the silk blouse and skirt, placing them gently out of reach of the sea. As the breeze caressed her flesh she hesitated, and then like a sleepwalker, removed her remaining articles of clothing, welcoming the silky embrace of the waves as she walked slowly into the sea.

She had never swum at night, nor completely unclad, come to that, and even now she was a little shocked at her own wanton impulsiveness, but the feel of the feel of the sea against her naked flesh was pleasurably erotic and she turned and floated, secure in the knowledge that the beach was private and that in any case the beaches of the Riviera held sufficient to satiate the male eye by day without the necessity of searching it out by night.

When she first saw the dark shadow on the small beach her heart almost stopped. She floated, almost motionless, while he walked to the small, betraying pile of clothes, and then slowly and purposefully removed his own, entering the sea with powerful strides, until the water was deep enough for him to swim towards her with unerring precision.

'Kieron.' His name was almost a whisper, her heightened senses telling her that this was not the time for words. She swam lazily away as he reached her, knowing that he would follow and that when he did he would catch her in mock struggle, dragging her down beneath the warm blue swell, to kiss her until sheer lack of oxygen forced them to the surface, trailing silver bubbles.

'What are you tonight?' he whispered against her ear. 'A mermaid? A siren, come to lure me to my doom?'

'Just a woman, Kieron,' she whispered back, twisting out from beneath his grasp and laughing like a child as she managed to elude his seeking hands. He could swim like a fish, far more powerfully than she could, and he circled her lazily as she turned back to the shore.

When they emerged from the sea, it seemed only natural that Kieron should lift her in his arms, without a word, and carry her to where the sea had washed clean a small patch of sand, placing her on it and covering her silver flesh with his own.

In complete silence, Briony lifted her hands to his face, tracing the hard bones, revelling in the feel of his warm, living flesh beneath her fingers, her breath coming unevenly between softly parted lips as his own hands began a lazy exploration of her skin.

She met his kiss eagerly and passionately, moaning softly as the hard pressure was suddenly removed after only the briefest, tormenting caress. A mouth as light as snow brushed gently against her skin, skimming briefly and leaving her aching for a more lasting contact.

Her hands moved feverishly against Kieron's body, as her lips pressed pleading kisses into his skin, her normal reticence and reserve sloughed off like an unwanted skin.

Kieron's flesh tasted of salt and sea, and he groaned huskily deep in his throat as she raised herself up against him, her breasts swelling passionately against his hair-darkened chest, the nipples tormented into hard erectness by the arousing contact. The soft warm curves of her body moulded themselves against his hardness, inciting him to take what she was offering and plummet them both deep into an endless whirlpool of shared passion.

There was no room for selfconsciousness or shame as Briony wound her arms possessively round his neck, holding his mouth against her as he tormented her with another brief caress, her sigh of satisfaction smothered under the fierce demand the action had aroused. When desire reached such a pitch, pain and pleasure mingled, she thought hazily, revelling in the hard possession of Kieron's hands on her flesh. This was no gentle, slow arousal to culminate in tender fulfilment, but a mutual primeval force akin to that of a storm-lashed ocean where each took demandingly from the other. Kieron's hands swept demandingly along her thigh, stroking over the tender skin of her stomach and upwards to caress her breast, the swelling flesh cupped by his hand, tormented by the rough caress of his tongue. Her harsh groan of pleasure as his mouth closed over the throbbing nipple was lost against his shoulder, her teeth clenching involuntarily on the tanned skin, eliciting a fevered response from the hands that held her slender moon-bathed body.

Kieron's withholding of their ultimate union was exquisitely unbearable, and Briony writhed feverishly beneath him, pleading implicitly for what he denied, her breath coming in soft, frenzied pants, her arms reaching up to pull him down against her.

Her clinging hands were removed, Kieron's body held away as he stared down at her aroused face and body.

'Now!' he said harshly, his breathing rasping and unsteady. 'Now tell me that you aren't all woman, Briony, and that you don't know what it feels like to want someone until you're *aching* with it.'

A cold fear was seeping over her. Kieron was no longer watching her with passion, but with a cold detachment that sent fear spiralling through her.

'Now I'm going to teach you something else,' he said softly, 'and I think you're going to be an excellent pupil, because I'm going to let you know what it feels like to be rejected the way you've constantly rejected me. And to do that I don't have to do a thing, do I, Briony?' he said cruelly. 'All I have to do is to walk away from you. No lovemaking without love, you once said to me, and that's exactly how I feel,' he said harshly. 'It was fun while it lasted, but now it's over.'

Without another word he turned and left her lying

on the sand, her mind in turmoil, while her body ached in bitter frustration and to her everlasting shame she knew beyond a shadow of a doubt that if he were to come back now and take her in his arms she would be powerless to resist him.

Somehow she managed to make her way to their room. There was no sign of Kieron, but then she had not expected that there would be. Her body throbbed with a deep hunger, which she tried to suppress. She had been so wrapped up in her own dreams, so exalted by what she had learned from Marian, that she had failed to appreciate the full effect of what, to Kieron, was her rejection, of both him and his love.

Of course he had wanted revenge. Hadn't she felt exactly the same? And forcing the 'woman' in her to respond to him was all part of that revenge. She knew enough about rejection to appreciate the bitterness and thirst for revenge which were its hydra-headed offspring. She should have talked to him, she thought drearily, explained that she had never had his letters, never known what had happened to him. But would it do any good? Wasn't his bitterness too deeply ingrained? If he had had the slightest shred of feeling left for her, surely tonight must have overcome the barriers.

A terrible weariness swept over her. She could go on no more. Tonight had drained every last drop of her courage. How could she even face Kieron again knowing how she had betrayed herself to him? No lovemaking without love, he had claimed, and yet he must have known how she felt, she had betrayed it so blatantly, wantonly encouraging him to make love to her. She groaned, turning over in the huge empty bed, beyond tears. Beyond anything but a need for total and absolute oblivion.

CHAPTER TEN

'I SEE you and Kieron were on the beach last night,' Louise announced acidly over breakfast.

Briony flushed but resolutely refused to look up from her croissants. Let Kieron answer her. Where had he been all night? To the best of her knowledge he had not returned to their room.

'You *were* on the beach, weren't you?' Louise pressed Kieron.

'Briony felt like a swim,' was all Kieron would say, but Briony's face flamed to think that Louise might have observed their lovemaking—or what had happened after.

During the morning Louise had a phone call from Paris, and returned to the patio with more animation in her face than Briony had previously observed.

'An old friend of mine from Paris,' she announced, flopping on to a sunlounger. 'Jean-Paul wants me to return home. What do you think, *chéri*?' she asked Kieron provocatively. 'Ought I to go?'

'That decision must surely rest only with you,' Marian said firmly. 'Jean-Paul has been very patient with you, Louise, but no man waits for ever, and from what your mother tells me he's a very successful and personable young man.'

Her words had obviously hit the right note, for after several minutes Louise excused herself and hurried into the salon, returning several minutes later to explain that she had booked herself on to the next Paris flight from Nice airport.

'Will you take me to the airport, *chéri*?' she pleaded to Kieron.

Briony excused herself, unwilling to witness the sight of the French girl openly attempting to seduce her husband. The pleasant breeze of the previous evening had turned into a spiteful wind, and her claim to have a headache was no lie. Even Nicky seemed querulous, and the temperature had dropped several degrees.

It was Héloise who explained what had happened when she brought Briony a soothing tisane.

'It is the mistral,' she said, shrugging her shoulders. 'It is the snake in what would otherwise be paradise,' she added fatalistically.

The tisane made Briony feel sleepy, her mind floating free of her body. She had no idea whether Kieron had taken Louise to the airport and neither did she care, or so she told herself. Had she learned nothing from the past? she asked herself resentfully. Once before she had hoped for love from Kieron Blake and not received it, so why had she thought it might be different a second time?

Her thoughts were too confusing and painful to be borne. She closed her eyes and let sleep take her in its protective embrace.

The silence awoke her, something in its empty quality alerting her to danger. Where was Nicky? It was long past the time for his rest, and surely Héloise would have woken her if she had put him to bed? Shivering with sudden inexplicable fear, Briony hurried into the small dressing room. One of Nicky's baby shoes lay discarded on the floor, his much beloved and chewed teddy-bear lying on the bed.

Telling herself that she was over-reacting, Briony

hurried into the kitchen. There was no sign of
Héloise, and biting her lip she remembered Marian
telling her that she usually gave Héloise and
François the same afternoon off.

'It means that François can take Héloise to see
her family and collect her again,' she explained to
Briony. 'He has some friends who run a bar and he
goes to see them.'

The empty kitchen sent her panic flaring again.
Where was everyone? Where was Nicky?

She went to Marian's room, expecting to find her
hostess resting, but the bed was smooth and untouched. 'Nicky!' She whimpered his name beneath
her breath, logic giving way to mindless fear as she
ran out of the house to the swimming pool, dreading
with every second discovering the lifeless body of her
child floating in its aquamarine waters.

The pool was empty and still.

Feverish and distraught, she searched the villa and
the gardens from top to bottom, calling Nicky's name
until she was hoarse. The others must all have gone out,
thinking Nicky was with his mother, where he would
have been if she hadn't been so selfishly wrapped up in
her own concerns. Tears burned her eyes, but she
refused to allow herself the luxury of letting them fall.

The wicket gate leading down to the beach caught
her eye and fresh dread seized her. Those steps so
narrow and dangerous were a sure lure for an ad-
venturous two-year-old.

She ran down them, ignoring the sharp grazes in-
flicted on her tender flesh, searching frantically along
the narrow shelving breach where the rocks met the
treacherous waters of the sea, sobbing Nicky's name
under her breath. Where was he? Alone and fright-

ened somewhere crying for her, or was he already beyond that? 'Please God, *no*!' The words were wrenched from white lips, her eyes huge with pain and terror, her breath coming in jerky uneven sobs as she stared out to sea.

There was no trace of the little boy.

She ran back to the villa, staring at the phone. Where was Kieron when she needed him? If only someone would appear! She could speak very little French and even if she managed to get in touch with the police how could she make herself properly understand? Where could Nicky have gone? He was such a *little* boy, barely able to walk for more than ten minutes without complaining that his legs ached. He was so infinitely precious; the most precious thing in her life, and yet through careless neglect she had lost him.

She heard the sound of a car and ran outside, her eyes widening in relief as she saw that it was Kieron's. He had started to turn the car round in a circle and hadn't seen her, and frantic with fear that he was going to leave, Briony flung herself despairingly in front of him, shuddering with pain as the bumper caught her slender body, and then through the scream of brakes and her own cry of pain she heard a car door swing open and Kieron's voice demanding harshly, 'You little fool, what are you trying to do? Kill yourself?'

She started to tell him about Nicky, but the words were lost, smothered in the thick stifling blanket which fell over her, her lips too numb and swollen for coherent speech.

Through tormented dreams she pursued Nicky, her breathing harsh and laboured, her body on fire with heat, always calling his name, but the little boy

eluded her. Once or twice Kieron appeared in the
dream, his expression accusing as he demanded to
know what she had done with his son, and although
she begged for his forgiveness it was never forthcoming. Sometimes she slipped back into the past when
there was no Nicky, only Kieron, and she awoke from
one of these dreams to find herself in her bed at the villa,
the sky dark velvet studded with diamond-bright stars.
Someone was sitting by her side, and she twisted her
head painfully, recognition and realisation flooding
over her as Kieron's dark blue eyes met hers.

'Nicky,' she moaned painfully, turning away.
'Where's Nicky. . . .?'

'Safe with Héloise,' Kieron told her abruptly, 'and
very worried about his mummy. What possessed you
to fling yourself in front of my car like that?'

'I couldn't find Nicky . . .' she shuddered with the
memory, 'and there was no one there. I. . . .' Weak
tears trickled down her face and she bit her lip
fiercely. Her body ached from the cuts and bruises
she must have sustained when she fell.

'He wasn't lost, you little fool,' Kieron said
roughly. 'I told Louise to tell you that we were
taking him with us to the airport to see the planes.'

'He was with you? All the time he was with you?'
Briony started to laugh, high hysterical laughter that
made it hurt to breathe, tears running unchecked
down her face. 'I didn't know . . . I never got your
message.'

'Not for the first time,' Kieron said enigmatically.
'Do you know you've been in a high fever for three days?'

'Have I?' She was curiously uninterested. 'Can I
see Nicky?' Her voice was urgent. 'Please, Kieron,
don't torment me! Please let me see him.'

'Of course I'm not going to torment you,' he replied harshly. 'I'll have Héloise bring him to you, and then you must try and sleep.'

Nicky was subdued but so plainly safe and well that she wanted to cry again. She ran her hands over his sturdy little body, and he tried to wriggle away, but she could not resist the desire to touch him and assure herself that she wasn't dreaming.

'Oh, darling,' she whispered huskily, hugging him to her, her eyes bright with tears as they met Kieron's across the room.

'Go with Héloise now, Nicky,' Kieron said calmly. 'Mummy needs to sleep.'

'Yes, I know. 'Cos she's been very, very ill!'

'I'm all better now, darling,' Briony said softly, releasing him to Héloise. It was long past his bedtime, but the Frenchwoman explained that the doctor had said that Briony might come out of her fever during the day and they had kept him up knowing she would want to see him.

'Why did you think I would want to punish you?' Kieron asked abruptly when they were alone. Briony had expected him to leave the room with Héloise and Nicky, but he had stayed, going to stand by the window where he had stared out to sea, before turning to confront her with the question.

'Did I?' she asked huskily, wetting her dry lips. 'I. . . .'

'In your dreams . . . during your fever. . . . It was constantly on your mind,' Kieron said harshly. 'You kept begging me to forgive you and pleading with me not to hurt you any more.'

'I was frightened you'd blame me for not taking proper care of Nicky,' Briony admitted breathlessly.

'Will you leave me now, please, Kieron? I . . . I'm . . . rather tired.'

She could not endure any more of his questions. If he continued to probe and press like this she would be bound to betray herself and admit that it had been his love and understanding she had been pleading for.

When he had gone she couldn't sleep. She had a shower and went back to bed, counting sheep until at last exhaustion claimed her.

She had the dream again. The one where she woke up and Kieron wasn't there, and in her fear and pain she called his name endlessly between her frantic sobs, unaware of the fact that she was not alone until she was shaken awake to find herself in Kieron's arms, his face drawn and harsh.

That he must have been in bed with her for some time was obvious, for the alarm clock showed three o'clock in the morning, and the bed held a heavy warmth which spoke of shared closeness of more than merely a few minutes.

'Briony. . . .'

'Don't touch me,' she sobbed bitterly, still held by the memory of the dream. 'You don't care about me, only Nicky holds your heart. . . .'

His hand was smoothing her hair back from her heated face, and it stilled suddenly, his eyes penetrating.

'And you want to?'

She froze from the question, her heart thudding under the hand he had slid down to cover it, one arm curving her against him so that she was resting against the strength of his body.

'Do you want to, Briony?' he prompted. 'Was that what it was all about down on the beach, mm?' His lips were touching her shoulder and her body ached to respond, but she remembered how he had cruelly rejected her and stared up at him with fear-shadowed eyes.

'Were you really giving me the gift of yourself, sweet Briony,' he whispered softly, 'and not just teasing as I thought?' There was a new deep timbre to his voice, his lips teased her skin gently.

Her body quivered against him, and although she tried to hide it from him she knew he had felt it. His tongue stroked gently along the delicate skin behind her ear, arousing all manner of delicious sensations, and her lips had to be clamped tightly together to prevent her small moan of pleasure escaping. His hands were stroking slowly along her body, pushing aside the thin silk of her nightgown and laying bare the satin flesh. His mouth touched her throat and then slid lower.

This time it was impossible to deny her reaction. Her throat ached with tension, her head falling back against the pillows as she begged him to stop.

He laughed softly, the sound feathering along her nerves. 'You don't really mean that, do you?' he murmured against her. 'That tantalising creature who came to me from the sea can't have disappeared entirely.' His arms wrapped round her, holding against his hardness, his mouth coaxing hers into slavish, mute subjugation as it parted for him.

His groaned satisfaction set off an answering chord deep inside her, and despite the promise she had made herself, never to betray her feelings to him again, she was reaching despairingly for him.

Her skin burned with fire, her mouth dry with tension. She touched the hard body with passionate demand, shuddering deeply as her fingers trembled over the flat hardness of his stomach, the powerful thighs and male loins pulsating so arousingly beneath her touch.

'Dear God, Briony,' Kieron protested harshly, pushing her away and substituting the soft warmth of her body for her straying hands, his arms clamping her to him, letting her know the effect her touch had had upon him.

'This time there's no turning back—for either of us,' he warned her on a fierce mutter, parting her thighs insistently. 'No teasing. No. . . .' He shuddered slightly, cupping her face, and fastening his mouth on her parted lips, draining its sweetness, the weight of his body pushing her into the bed and keeping her there, while the deep agonising ache inside her built up to a crescendo of intensity.

'Love me, Kieron,' she moaned huskily against his throat, her skin hectically flushed. 'Don't leave me this time. Don't stop. . . .'

His fingers tangled in her hair, his breathing harsh and laboured, the first moment of possession unbearably sweet as he stroked and enticed her body into melting surrender, the pleasure intensified by his unhurried response to her plea for complete fulfilment.

There was a moment when she thought he was going to withdraw from her, and she arched against him frantically, her arms clinging to his shoulders, but his hoarse, 'It's all right, darling . . . it's all right, Briony,' soothed her, and then his hardness possessed her completely, her gasped pleasure stifled against his mouth, his husky, 'Let me have you completely, Briony, body and soul,' sending her frantic with a desire which was only satiated when the world burst

into flames around them, and Briony floated peacefully
thousands of miles from earth on a cloud of pure heaven.

'Did you enjoy that, darling?'

The words reached her from a distance, and she
cringed faintly from them.

'You wanted me,' Kieron reminded her, 'just like
you did on the beach.'

On the beach! That recalled things she would far
rather forget. 'That was different!' He had made love
to her, but there was still so much unresolved between them.

The words were wrung from her, and Kieron
cupped her face with his hands, his eyes searching it
intently, feature by feature, lingering longest on her
trembling mouth.

'Why? Because Tante Marian had just told you
about my illness? Oh yes, I know. She told me while
you were ill. Is that what melted the barriers, Briony?
Is that why you responded to me so passionately?'

His thumb was stroking her throat, and she tried
to escape the small caress. Even now after their lovemaking her body was still frighteningly responsive to
him.

'You already know why I did,' Briony responded
tightly. 'It was all part of your plan to reveal the
"woman" in me, wasn't it? And then to reject me
like. . . .'

'Like I thought you'd rejected me?' Kieron
prompted. 'Is that what you thought? Is that what
you're thinking now?'

There was a long silence when she felt totally unable
to speak, and Kieron moved restlessly against her.

'Do you really want to know the truth?' he asked
at last.

Her throat was a tight ball of pain. She nodded, willing herself to endure whatever he said.

'When you came to me out of the sea like that I thought you were the sexiest, most desirable thing I'd ever seen, and then, the way you responded to me.... I thought I must be going out of my mind.... Do you know how long I've dreamed of having you like that?' he demanded savagely. 'God, Briony, all through those months in Africa, and then when I got back and was so ill. I came very close to hating you then, my love. I could understand you being bitter, but I never thought you would reject me totally. I told myself I could forget you. I was offered a job in America and leapt at the chance. London was too tempting. I could easily have found myself haunting your flat, begging for crumbs from your table. And then I came back, and damn near the first thing I see is you, but you'd changed. You were cold, and more infuriating, you seemed to think I was the one who ought to be suffering from guilt. You were so hard and cold, I couldn't believe you meant it when you accused me of making you like that. I thought you were just trying to make me feel bad, and then I found out about Nicky and it all seemed to make sense. This was your revenge for my leaving you with a child. But by then it was too late anyway, I was as hooked as I'd ever been. It wasn't just for the Myers story back then—you must try to believe that. I wanted you very badly, my darling, but I couldn't confide in you. There was no way you were capable of concealing the truth from Susan Myers, so I told myself that once it was all over I would explain and that we'd laugh about it together once we were married. You gave yourself to me so sweetly, I couldn't believe it when you rejected me. I didn't marry you solely for possession of my son, Briony. I could have got that through the courts. No, I knew the moment I set eyes on you again that I had to have you, no matter what the cost, and then once we were married it wasn't enough, I wanted to turn you into the warm, loving girl you'd been before. . . .'

'I thought you were just tormenting me.'

'I know—now. When Aunt Marian told me that you'd never had my letters I thought you must be lying, and then I asked myself why you would— what would be the point?'

'Susan Myers must have taken your letter,' Briony whispered. His hands were stroking over her ribs, cupping and moulding her breasts and suddenly she no longer wanted to talk.

'I thought that you'd just left me, Kieron, and I was so bitter. We'd made love and it was the most beautiful thing that had ever happened to me. I kept fantasising about how you would come back, but you never did, and then there was the scandal, and when I discovered about Nicky. . . . I was so hurt to think that you would never see him, never know what a perfect child we had made together.'

'I thought when I married you that eventually you might come to love me again. . . .'

'I never stopped,' Briony confessed, nuzzling his shoulder. 'I told myself I had, but I was lying. When Marian told me what had really happened, and I knew that you had loved me, I could think only of that, I thought if I let you see how I felt, we could overcome the past, but I'd forgotten that you too would be bitter. . . .'

'And so you gave yourself to me like a sea sacrifice,' Kieron said gently, 'and I tormented you, spurning your precious gift. . . .' His lips brushed her ear. 'Would the sea give me a second chance, do you suppose?'

In the darkness, Briony stared at him. 'You mean. . . .'

'I mean a re-enactment of the sea god's gift, but this time, my darling, I promise you it will be properly received. Not now, but when you feel that you can trust yourself entirely to me, when you have truly forgiven me, we can wipe out the bitterness of the past and. . . . Where are you going?' he demanded harshly as she slid off the bed.

She paused and smiled mischievously over her shoulder, pure Eve, and deliberately tantalising.

'Where do you think?' she said provocatively. 'I suddenly have this strange desire to swim.'

The look in Kieron's eyes as he reached for her assured her beyond any doubt how he felt about her, even before she heard his husky words of love.

'For ever, and for always,' he assured her shudderingly as he lifted her hands to kiss the soft palms in tender worship.

'As I love you,' Briony murmured unsteadily.

All at once she couldn't wait to be on the beach, the same tide that drove the sea eternally against the shore rising slowly inside her. Her hands trembled in Kieron's, the glow in her eyes lighting an answering fire in his, and with a sudden prescience she knew that tonight she would conceive the child which would be Nicky's brother—or sister.

A faint smile curved her lips. A gift not from the gods, but from her husband—a gift of life; a gift of love.

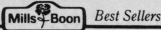 *Best Sellers*

YOU'RE INVITED TO ACCEPT
2 BEST SELLER ROMANCES
AND A TOTE BAG
 **FREE!**

Acceptance card

| NO STAMP NEEDED | Post to: Reader Service, FREEPOST, P.O. Box 236, Croydon, Surrey. CR9 9EL |

Please note readers in Southern Africa write to:
Independant Book Services P.T.Y., Postbag X3010, Randburg 2125, S. Africa

YES! Please send me 2 free Best Seller Romances and my free tote bag – and reserve a Reader Service Subscription for me. If I decide to subscribe I shall receive 4 new Best Seller Romances every other month as soon as they come off the presses for £4.40 together with a FREE newsletter including information on top authors and special offers, exclusively for Reader Service subscribers. There are no postage and packing charges, and I understand I may cancel or suspend my subscription at any time. If I decide not to subscribe I shall write to you within 10 days. Even if I decide not to subscribe the 2 free novels and the tote bag are mine to keep forever. I am over 18 years of age   EP21B

NAME _____
                                            (CAPITALS PLEASE)

ADDRESS _____

_____

_____ POSTCODE _____

The right is reserved to refuse application and change the terms of this offer. You may be mailed with other offers as a result of this application. Offer expires March 31st 1988 and is limited to one per household.
Offer applies in UK and Eire only. Overseas send for details.

Two lives, two destinies

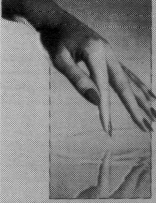

WORLDWIDE

Reflection

Two lives, two destinies – but was one
a chilling reflection of the other?

Andrew Neiderman

–but the same fate?

Cynthia Warner discovers frightening similarities
between her own life and that of Karla Hoffman. Even
down to the same marriage difficulties they experience.
   The one alarming exception is that Karla was murdered
in Cynthia's house 50 years before.
   Is Cynthia destined to suffer the same fate?

An enthralling novel by Andrew Neiderman
Available December 1987 Price £2.95

W🌐RLDWIDE

Available from Boots, Martins, John Menzies, W H Smith,
Woolworths and other paperback stockists.